NavPress Publishing Group
P.O. Box 35001, Colorado Springs, Colorado 80935

The Navigators is an international Christian organization. Jesus Christ gave His followers the Great Commission to go and make disciples (Matthew 28:19). The aim of The Navigators is to help fulfill that commission by multiplying laborers for Christ in every nation.

NavPress is the publishing ministry of The Navigators. NavPress publications are tools to help Christians grow. Although publications alone cannot make disciples or change lives, they can help believers learn biblical discipleship, and apply what they learn to their lives and ministries.

Library of Congress Catalog Card Number to be assigned.
ISBN 08910-98658

Cover illustration: Dan Craig

The stories and characters in this book are fictitious. Any resemblance to people living or dead is coincidental.

Printed in the United States of America

1 2 3 4 5 6 7 8 9 10 11 12 13 14 15 / 00 99 98 97 96 95

CONTENTS

To Tim,
when my pen writes it writes of you
for you have made divine love palpable
and set my spirit free
like a swan on the wind

1
THE SMILING SWAN

Margaret balanced herself for a moment on the swinging bridge so she could hoist her book bag a bit higher onto her shoulder. After glancing quickly behind her she grabbed the roped railing on either side of the bridge and hastily began stepping from one wet wooden plank to the next. With dismay she noticed that one of her sneakers was untied. She didn't have time to stop and fix it now. She would just have to be careful not to trip, for she had a dreadful feeling *they* were gaining on her. About halfway across the bridge Margaret froze. The knuckles on her hand turned white as she tightened her grip around the railing. From behind her the silence of the woods was broken by a crackling and then a loud snapping of branches. Two skinny boys in denim jeans and T-shirts marked with sweat burst from the tangled brush and stood on the bank breathing heavily. They spotted Margaret almost at once and grinned in response to her narrow glare.

"There she is!" screamed the shorter one, Craig, in his high-pitched, nasal voice, jumping and pointing. "We've found her, Ryan!"

Craig gave a hoot and began dancing around in circles like a warrior. (Margaret thought he looked more like a monkey.) Ryan reached into his jacket pocket to reveal something that was bright blue, round, and shook like Jell-O. Margaret could see that it was a water balloon. Ryan began tossing the blubbery blue balloon from one hand to the other.

"We've found her! We've found the runt with the braces and braids!" Craig sang up to her.

"Don't fall, Margaret," Ryan taunted, walking toward the concrete steps that led to the bridge. "Don't fall, Margaret, you might get wet!"

"Yeah," agreed Craig, wiping his nose with the back of his hand and following along. "Drenched!"

Margaret decided to keep walking and ignore them for as long as she could. They really were immature. Unfortunately, she managed to take only a few more steps before Craig and Ryan burst onto the bridge. With a wild yell they began jumping up and down making the bridge buckle and swing in violent spasms. They yelled and hooted at her, but Margaret was too intent on keeping her balance to hear what they were saying. She tried to continue walking, as she was still a good distance from them, but it was hard to move without jolting forward. The bridge swayed and buckled under her, and she was afraid if she tried to go anywhere she'd slip out from underneath the rope.

"You guys better quit it!" Margaret yelled back at them. "It's not funny! I could get killed, you know!"

"Gee whiz, no, Margaret," Ryan said, pausing momentarily from his stampede. "You'd just get wet."

"Besides," declared Craig in a high-pitched whine, wiping his nose again, "if you did fall in you wouldn't die. Ryan and me, we dove off here last week on that real hot day, and we didn't die—did we, Ryan?"

"Quiet, Craig!" Ryan ordered. "I'm about ready to use my ammunition on the runt with the braids. On three we'll charge. Ready?"

"You guys better cut it out!" demanded Margaret again. She had not moved an inch and was clinging to the railing for dear life. "I'll tell Mrs. Grafton!"

"Gee whiz, I'm scared," Ryan feigned. "Aren't you scared, Craig? After all, Margaret, you're so full of lies and bad grades I'm sure the teacher will believe you."

"I am not!"

"Anyway, we want you to learn a lesson."

"Right!" Craig echoed in a hollow voice.

Ryan drew back the hand that held the blue water balloon.

"So on three we charge her. Ready? One . . . two . . . three!"

Margaret closed her eyes and held on to the roped railing with all her might. Let them throw their old balloon and get it over with. She'd show them (when she was on firmer ground, of course) not to mess with her! She heard them galloping toward her and felt the bridge surge and swing. Opening her eyes to keep her balance she saw the water balloon jerkily wing its way toward her in the air. She turned her back and covered her face. At the same moment a staccato cry followed a loud splash. The water balloon smashed open at her feet. Margaret swung around and saw only Ryan looking at her wide-eyed and motionless. All was silent. Neither she nor Ryan moved or spoke. For a stunning instant they stood staring at one another with their mouths open.

"He slipped," Ryan whispered finally. "Right out from under the rope."

Margaret balked. No words came out. Both leaned over the rope desperately scanning the water for Craig's blond head. At any moment, Margaret assured herself, she would see him come bobbing to the surface.

"Hey, Craig!" Ryan ventured nonchalantly at the river after a few moments of silence. "Stop hiding and come on up. We know you're down there."

"He's down there all right," Margaret hissed.

"He should be up soon," predicted Ryan cooly. "He's not a strong swimmer, but he can stay afloat. He did fine last week when we dove off of here. He came right up, laughing and sputtering."

Suddenly Ryan had become very personable. They waited. The water in the river was high from the rain—almost level with the muddy bank on either side. Because of the heavy volume, it was moving more quickly than usual, tossing up bits of spray and foam as it skidded over the top of large rocks hugging the bank's perimeter. Still there was no sign of Craig. A full minute went by. Margaret felt a dreadful panic rising in her throat as if someone were strangling her.

"He's not coming up," she breathed faintly after a few more seconds had elapsed.

Ryan looked at her with a blank expression as if he didn't understand.

"Hey, c'mon, Craig!" he shouted into the river. "Gee whiz, enough is enough. You're scaring us!"

Margaret was desperate. "Don't you get it? He's not coming up. Get with it and do something!"

She scrambled to the end of the bridge, jumped the stairs, and threw her book bag on the ground. Then she kicked off her shoes and dove into the water. This second splash awakened Ryan from a daze. He descended from the bridge in a frenzy and dove in after Margaret.

Both of them were fair swimmers and together they searched frantically, diving into the brown water again and again. It was impossible to see anything in the mire. Occasionally both of them would surface together and look hopefully at the other only to dive under again clawing desperately at the darkness. The current was strong and the children finally collapsed exhausted on the slimy bank a good distance downstream from where they had begun. They were coughing and heaving as if their lungs were going to burst.

"Someone has got to go for help!" Margaret panted, gulping for air.

"I'll go," said Ryan mechanically, staggering to his feet. His wet clothes clung like plastic wrap to his body.

"It's shorter if you go toward my house than if you try to go to town," Margaret managed hoarsely. "It's only about half a mile to my house."

A fragrant breeze blew lightly across Margaret's face.

"You needn't bother," said a regal voice from downstream.

Both children looked at each other to make sure they had heard correctly.

"Who's there?" yelled Ryan desperately in the direction of the voice. "Who is it? Help us please! We need your help."

There was no response. Only the sound of the tireless river met their ears, brimming and surging forward in constant motion and finally disappearing around a bend beyond their sight.

"Someone's drowned," yelled Margaret rising to her feet. "Don't go away; help us, please!"

Heavy tears filled her eyes, making everything foggy and out of focus. When she tried to yell, her throat was too tight.

"No one has drowned," the voice sounded back.

"Yes, they have!" screamed Ryan, "A friend of ours. His name is Craig!" Again there was no answer. This time another light breeze blew across their faces and brought with it the most alluring smell of pine and lilac. Margaret did not remember ever having seen lilacs growing in this part of the wood before, although pine trees flourished in abundance along the river's edge.

"Whoever it was is gone," declared Ryan after a moment's pause.

"You'd think they'd help," Margaret said testily, smearing a tear across her face with the palm of her hand. "It seems to me we're wasting time. Why are you just standing there? I ought to punch you out for all of this. It's all your fault, this whole blasted mess!"

"Oh, so it's my fault, is it?" Ryan challenged, raising himself up to his full gangly height. Margaret thought he resembled a stalk of asparagus when he stood straight up because his hair always came to a point at the top. "You're the one who came into these disgusting woods in the beginning. I've got mosquito bites and scratches all over my arms. Whoever heard of walking home this way?"

"So? Maybe if you hadn't been chasing me all the way from the school yard I wouldn't have come this way, and maybe if you hadn't jumped all over the bridge Craig wouldn't be. . . ."

She couldn't say the word *drowned*. She collapsed onto the muddy bank and put her head in her hands. To think that Craig was lying dead somewhere, that they would find him limp and white, washed up on a rock downstream was too much to bear. She could see Craig's mother, that massive woman, crying—little round tears journeying down those lardy plains of cheek. And the two of them, Ryan and Margaret, at the funeral, dressed in black and grounded for life. Rev. Mills would be preaching, and she might have to get up and say a few words about Craig, the wispy, spidery son of a bakery woman and a farmer. *Someone should have taken a tissue to his nose more often*, Margaret thought ruefully.

"No one is dead," came the voice assuredly. Margaret lifted her head and wiped more stray tears from her cheeks. Ryan, who had already begun sprinting away, stopped short and rushed to the edge of the bank trying to peer around the bend in the river.

"Who are you?" Margaret demanded huskily. The faintest smell of pine and lilac drifted past. This time, although there was no answer, a soft breeze stirred the leaves in the nearby trees. Then, as if summoned by the breeze, around the bend glided into view the most enormous white swan either of them had ever seen. The swan was swimming effortlessly upriver, and as it grew closer both children gawked. Sprawled across the swan's back, his head resting against the base of the arched serpentine neck, was a motionless Craig. Both the swan and Craig were dappled in sunlight that had suddenly burst through a hole in the clouds.

The swan was swimming quite rapidly, and in moments it was only a few feet away from them. Both children began to blink and squint as it came closer. This was not only because they were astounded at seeing Craig astride the swan's back but because of the flickering colors that emanated from the water in the area where the bird was swimming. Wherever the swan went it floated in a halo of reds, greens, golds, and a kind of bluish purple. The colors danced around the swan's body and flashed rays of light now and then that were too brilliant for the children's eyes—as a flashbulb might stun the eyes for a moment when a photograph is taken.

The more they gazed upon the swan, however, the more they found their eyes growing accustomed to the movement of the light and color as it played on the water and they found it easier to focus on the swan's face. Neither of them cowered at the sight of this awesome creature. Perhaps it was because of the relief they felt at seeing Craig again or because the swan's presence was genuinely personable, if one can say that about a bird. When they did manage to focus on the bird's face it was clear to both Ryan and Margaret that the bird was smiling. It made no sense when they sat and talked about it later, for birds don't smile. Everyone knows that all birds have beaks that are not malleable; they wear the same expression all the time whether they're twittering or chirping or singing or pulling up a worm or diving for a fish, because their mouths are made out of bone. That's not to say that birds don't want to smile. Margaret was sure that they did when she used to watch them feeding at the bird feeder her mother hung for her on the back porch. She used to think it rather sad that birds could sing and not smile. However, this bird—well it was quite clear there was a smile on its beak, even though it might sound impossible. The best Margaret and Ryan could do to describe it to themselves later was that when the bird smiled, the posture of its neck changed from a regal arch to a low bow in order to gain eye contact with them.

"Greetings!" declared the swan, paddling much closer to the bank so that it was only about three feet away. From the tone of its voice the swan seemed to be under the impression that he knew them quite well. "I found your friend floating downriver. I thought I should return him to you."

"Gee whiz . . . yes . . . yes, of course," Ryan stammered awkwardly.

"Craig's sleeping quite peacefully now, as you can see," continued the swan happily, as if oblivious to Ryan's stammering. "He was a bit chilled when I picked him up. In fact, he was shaking a good deal. So it was simply a matter of fluffing up my down. He's toasty warm now."

"Yes, of course," Ryan repeated, still too stunned to be good company. This swan knew Craig's name. "Gee whiz, are you for real, or is this some kind of joke?"

"What Ryan means is that we're both very grateful," blurted out Margaret, not wanting to offend the creature and lose Craig in the process. "We thought, well, that Craig had drowned."

"I know, Margaret," sighed the swan. "You did an admirable job looking for him. It's just that when one is born and raised in the water it's easier to maneuver. You often see things that landbred creatures miss."

"So you were spying on us?" queried Ryan.

"You don't have to spy on people to know about them," said the swan with dignity arching his neck.

"I only thought for a moment . . ." Ryan began, his face flushing.

"It's quite all right," assured the swan.

"Excuse me," Margaret interjected somewhat confused, "you seem to know us, but we don't know you at all."

"It's a pity," agreed the swan.

"Do you mind telling us your name then? I mean, if you have one."

"Of course I have a name!" the swan piped back at her, obviously thrilled that she had asked. He lowered his neck once more and spoke quietly as if dispensing a treasured piece of information.

"My name is Laurel."

The late afternoon sun shone brilliantly through the trees and the dancing colors in the water took on a golden hue.

"That's a nice name," Ryan responded guiltily, hoping the swan still liked him.

"It's a lovely name," agreed Margaret, crouching down to gain eye contact with him. "We are very pleased to meet you, Laurel. Are there more swans like you downriver?"

Laurel's large, dark eyes looked longingly toward the sky and Margaret thought they grew moist.

"No, dear," the swan responded ever so slowly after a lengthy pause. "There are no other swans like me downriver. I'm afraid I am here alone, on assignment, if you can understand my drift. Pardon the pun, of course."

"Of course," chimed in Ryan, still feeling guilty. He didn't know what a pun was.

Laurel gazed wistfully at the sky for a moment longer and then shivered a bit and recovered.

"You are welcome, of course, to use my name whenever you might need it."

Laurel said this with the pleasure one would use to propose a toast or present a gift to a dear friend. Neither Margaret nor Ryan knew what the swan meant, but Laurel appeared satisfied and continued.

"And now, about this boy on my back. You do want him, don't you?"

Both children nodded vigorously.

"Would you mind doing me a bit of a favor and lifting him off? I can feel his breath on my neck and it is getting more shallow. He will be waking up shortly and it's best he be on land when he does so he won't roll into the water."

The swan came close to the shoreline and the water flashed brilliant colors at the children's faces. Margaret remembered reaching out for Craig to lift him up and seeing Ryan right beside her. And then everything went black.

2

UNCLE JOHN CHANGES HIS MIND

Margaret woke to find Uncle John tucking an afghan under her feet. The first thing she noticed was how gray her uncle's face was. Even his mouth was a small, thin line. She heard the clattering of dishes and realized she was not in bed but lying on the couch in the living room. Everything was fuzzy and dreamy. Then she heard her uncle say, "She's awake!" The dishes stopped clanging in the kitchen, and soon two faces were peering down at her. The pudgy, round face on her right was Auntie Emily, who was visiting from New York City. She was so short she could barely see over the back of the couch.

"Auntie? Is that you . . ." Margaret's mouth wouldn't move right.

"You're darn tootin' it's me," the voice shot back. "You ought to be tarred and feathered."

"It's good to see you awake, Margaret," said Uncle John softly.

He was sitting on the edge of the couch holding her hand. Margaret thought he looked sad.

"You!" began Auntie Emily, pointing her index finger

at Margaret. She came around from the back of the couch and stood at Margaret's feet. She was shaking her finger so hard it looked bendy like rubber.

"You," said Auntie Emily again, "are a very impudent, disobedient young lady. You had both of us worried sick. Why, when you came to the door an hour ago you just about collapsed on the floor. And you were so covered with mud you messed up the carpet it just took me three hours to clean! Your uncle was about ready to call the police to go look for you. I don't understand it. If you belonged to me I'd fetch the paddle and you'd be over my knee right this minute."

"Emily, please calm down," John cautioned quietly.

"I've told you before, and I tell you now, John Morrison, you're too good to that child," Emily shot back.

Auntie Emily's mannerisms, although brazen, cleared Margaret's head almost at once. What had happened at the river suddenly thrust itself with horror on her consciousness. She remembered waking up under a pine tree on the river bank as it was growing dark and stumbling home. She sat bolt upright on the couch.

"Craig! What about Craig?" She scanned her uncle's face hoping to read his expression before he told her the terrible news. John only shrugged.

"He's fine. His mom called us before you got here to let us know what had happened. He told his mom he almost drowned and that you and Ryan were with him at the time. We were about ready to go out and look for you when you arrived home. We were very worried about you, Margaret. I'm not sure you realize how worried."

Margaret looked from one face to the other. They were not hiding the truth from her just to be kind. Auntie Emily would have said it if it were true. Craig was all right.

"Laurel," whispered Margaret under her breath.

"What was that?" John bent closer to hear.

"Water," said Margaret quickly. "I need some water."

Auntie Emily huffed and puffed her way into the kitchen and came back with some ice water in a glass with a flexi-straw. The phone rang as it always did around supper time and Uncle John went to answer it.

"May I make a phone call, please?" she asked her aunt when she returned.

"You are to rest, young lady, and not get up and start causing trouble again! Your uncle has something to discuss with you that is not going to be pleasant, I can assure you," Auntie Emily snipped. "Drink your water! I didn't bring it so you could stare at it."

Margaret took a sip of water and resigned herself to being punished. She knew she was not supposed to walk home through the woods after school, but she hardly gave the nature of her punishment a second thought. The only thing that mattered was Craig. With him alive, nothing that was done to her would matter. The thought foremost in her mind was that enormous swan and whether or not it was real. She knew she needed to talk to Ryan, and quickly. Maybe it was all a dream. But *if, just maybe, if* he had seen Laurel also, then she would know that beautiful swan wasn't just pretend. None of these grown people had a belief in things that were extraordinary. Uncle John was a physician and far too scientific and serious. Mrs. Grafton, her teacher at school, was scientific too. She said you could prove facts in test tubes and with numbers. She said that when you did that you knew something was true *empirically*. Margaret never had a need for test tubes and numbers because she already knew things were true just because they were—like that swan. Then there was Auntie Emily, who was probably the most negative person Margaret had ever met and who never believed anything anyone said that was good anyway. She'd been visiting for a week and was leaving in two days. Margaret couldn't wait! All grown people tended to doubt things, though, especially good things. Margaret was convinced she didn't want to live past age sixteen. After that point everyone got too boring because they had figured out everything that was possible and impossible. The weird thing was that grown people usually thought most bad things were possible and most good things impossible.

Margaret wished her mother were still alive. Her mother would have believed her. Her mother had always believed in impossible things. She used to write stories about elves, fairies, unicorns, secret passageways, and magic lands. She used to read them to Margaret at bedtime. Margaret had been the official "tester" of the stories. Margaret's job, her mother had always told her, was to see if the impossible seemed possible. If Margaret believed the stories were possible, her mother would send them away. Sometimes they would be published in a magazine somewhere.

Her mother had died in a car accident a year ago. That's when Margaret had come to live with Uncle John. Uncle John had been kind and gentle, even if he did always look a little sad. He had often held her when she would become terrified at night, crying out in her sleep and moaning. He would hold her then and rock her in the big, bulky quilt by the fire as if she were a tiny baby. He would rock her until all her tears were gone and she fell asleep with her head against his shoulder. Margaret fingered the locket around her neck where she had placed her mother's picture. Yes, her mother would have believed in Laurel. Most definitely. In fact, she probably would have written a story about the swan. *Anyway*, thought Margaret, bringing herself back to the present, *there was only one way to find out what was real and what wasn't. Ryan would be her "tester."*

"I need to call Ryan," she blurted out. "Please, Auntie Emily! I'll only be a second!"

Auntie Emily glared at Margaret from the kitchen, but before she could say anything Uncle John appeared in the living room and beckoned to Margaret with his index finger.

"If you're up, you might as well come into the study, Margaret. Let's get this over with."

Uncle John walked ahead of her into the study. It was the place where they always had their "talks" when something went wrong. Margaret wrapped the afghan tightly around her shoulders and followed dutifully behind him. She felt her aunt's piercing gaze follow her. Finally she closed the heavy study door behind her with relief. Uncle John fished about on his desk for his pipe and some tobacco. He motioned to his niece to sit in the big, overstuffed easy chair with the pillows. It was the kind of chair that reclined easily enough, so, without meaning to, Margaret soon found herself lying on her back and staring at the ceiling. It took several tries before she managed to jerk the chair into an upright position again.

"It's been a tough year, Margaret, hasn't it?" he began, settling himself into the couch opposite her. "This incident really tops them all though, Margaret. I can't remember when I've been so worried."

"I'm sorry," Margaret responded humbly. "I'm sorry for going into the woods. I'm sorry for causing all of this trouble, and you can do anything to me that you like as punishment."

John pressed the tobacco into his pipe and lit it.

"Margaret, this involves more than just a simple reprimand or punishment. You could have been killed out there. The river was extremely high after the rain. You're not supposed to go into those woods. What got into you?"

"Well," Margaret began slowly, measuring her words. "The boys were chasing me with a water balloon out of school, so I ran into the woods to the swinging bridge thinking that I would lose them on the way, but I didn't. And that's it."

"Uh huh," said John puffing smoke into the air and looking at her with raised eyebrows. "And what happened then?"

Margaret sank further into the chair and hugged the pillow.

"Margaret," continued John slowly, "I am sending you back to New York City with your Auntie Emily. It will be good for you."

"What?" Margaret's jaw dropped open not wanting to comprehend.

"You're not happy here, Margaret, I can see that," her uncle continued calmly, forcing a weak smile. (It looked really fake because John rarely smiled.) You're not doing well in school, you're always in fights, you've lied to me and to your teacher. To make matters worse, I can't keep track of your whereabouts. If anything should ever happen to you I would never forgive myself. I know Auntie Emily is rather prickly and old-fashioned, but perhaps, in a more familiar environment you'll come through this difficult time more easily. Just think, you can go to your old school, be with your old friends, and do things the way you used to. I'll still be your guardian, but this way you would be able to live in your old neighborhood, and maybe it would be easier for you."

Margaret felt as if there were a bomb in her chest about ready to go off. It took her two seconds to throw the afghan and the pillows to the floor and stand before her uncle. Her fists were clenched, her eyes livid.

"I never thought," she began haltingly between clenched teeth, "that you would do this. I trusted you."

"Margaret please . . ." John began, "I want you to be happy. That's all."

"I won't be happy with Auntie Emily!"

"How do you know?" asked John searching her face and putting his pipe down. "She's a woman and she knows about girl things. I don't. I'm just a bachelor. I've got a doctor's schedule. I'm no match for a little girl."

"She's no woman, she's a witch!" Margaret declared brazenly. "I hate her and I hate you, too!"

She tried to run away, but her uncle sprang forward and held her firmly by the shoulders.

"Margaret, I told myself that if you told me the truth today about what happened I might change my mind. You didn't, and that's that. I can't let your life go on like this. Your mother wouldn't have wanted it this way for you either."

"My mother wouldn't have sent me away," Margaret challenged defiantly, tears running freely down her cheeks. "You wouldn't believe me anyway, even if I had told you what really happened."

"What really happened, Margaret?"

"You won't believe me. I know you won't!"

"Try me," persisted John again. He was trying to look his niece in the eye, but Margaret had her eyes stonily focused on the braided rug.

"Okay," she dared him after a moment's pause, sucking in her breath and meeting her uncle's tired gaze. "It was Craig who fell in the water, okay? Ryan and I went in after him and couldn't find him and a magic swan rescued him on his back and talked to us and told us what our names were. See, I told you that you wouldn't believe me!"

She had managed to say it all in one breath and so quickly that John blinked a couple of times in rapid succession. He let go of his niece's shoulders and put the pipe back in his mouth. Then he quietly surveyed Margaret for a long moment. Finally he sat back and began gesturing as if twirling the ends of his bristly short moustache that wouldn't twirl.

"A magic swan you say, Margaret?"

The lines in John's face had softened a little.

"That's what I said," she mumbled, looking again at the rug. She knew she was doomed now. How could Uncle John believe in a magic swan? There was no escaping spending her days in Auntie Emily's dark air shaft apartment that smelled of powder and mildew.

"And how did this magic swan rescue Craig?"

"The swan had Craig on his back. He swam upriver and that's all I remember, except he could talk."

Margaret figured she had nothing to lose at this point.

"I see," said her uncle pensively. "The swan talked to you?"

He had a puzzled frown on his face.

"Margaret," John continued, "are you sure this isn't one of your mother's stories that you're remembering?"

Margaret nodded. She continued to stare at the braided rug and dug her big toe into it. It was useless. Uncle John was thirty-three and too scientific. She reached up and fingered the locket on her neck and said nothing. John put his finger under Margaret's chin and lifted her head up. Margaret finally met his gaze.

"It could have been a dream," she admitted slowly, "but I don't think so."

"I see," said John again.

There was another long pause. Finally, John cleared his throat.

"All right, I admit it. Maybe I made the wrong decision. I didn't think you'd be so upset. I really didn't think you wanted to stay with me in a strange, small town with all the problems you've been having in school. I thought you might be glad to go back. I really did."

Margaret looked suspiciously at her uncle.

"So I can stay then?"

"We'll try again," sighed her uncle shaking his head. "But you have to promise me something."

"What's that?" Margaret asked, wiping stray tears away with the back of her hand. John fumbled in his pocket for a handkerchief, found it, and dabbed at his niece's cheeks.

"That you'll be honest with me. No more lies. I have to be able to trust you."

"No more lies," Margaret agreed. "So you believe me, then? About the swan, I mean."

John didn't answer right away, and he gazed past her as if remembering something.

"Never mind that, Margaret. I believe that you believe you are telling the truth. I don't know what I believe right now. I don't even know if I'm doing the best thing for you, but we shall see."

Margaret looked at her uncle's tired face. "I don't really hate you," she said in a husky voice. "I'm sorry I said that. And I don't want to go and live with anyone else but you."

"We shall see," John said again. "I'm afraid I have to

ground you for a while. You weren't supposed to be walking home that way."

Margaret nodded brightly. Oh! To see her aunt's face when she learned that Margaret was staying . . . what a trip! But her uncle was still talking and she knew she would not be afforded that pleasure.

"Go up and change for bed. I'll be up in a minute."

Margaret walked slowly to the door where she paused uncertainly. Perhaps she could be in on it if she tried a bit of tactful persuasion.

"Uncle John?"

"Yes?"

"What about Auntie Emily?"

"I'll explain it all to her with a few compliments. She'll be fine."

"Uncle John?"

"Yes?"

"Shouldn't I be there when you tell her that I'm staying here and everything? I mean you might need me to help explain things."

"I'm sure I can handle it, Margaret. Thank you."

"Are you sure?"

"I'm sure. Go get ready for bed."

"Uncle John?"

"What is it, Margaret?"

Margaret had intended on begging him some more, but instead she found different words coming out of her mouth.

"Do you often think about my mother?"

"I think about Annie every day," said John haltingly. "You look just like her, Margaret. Especially your big brown eyes. Now go upstairs."

Margaret slipped out quietly leaving the door slightly ajar. John sat pensively for a minute. Then he stood up and began searching for something in his bookcase. When he found it he pulled it out almost reverently. It was a large, navy blue volume with gold cursive on the front that read "Scrapbook." Slowly he began turning the yellowed pages scanning each carefully. Some of the pages had writing on them, others had items glued to them like fall leaves pressed in waxed paper and old photographs. As he neared the end of the book, he stopped abruptly at a large pencil sketch taped across each corner of the paper and down the sides. The tape had yellowed and the pencil lines had blurred and smudged a bit. In the bottom left hand corner the name "Annie" was written in childish scrawl with the word "Laurel" directly underneath. The sketch was a picture of an enormous swan, and the swan was smiling.

3
THE MEETING

The next morning, in her locker at school, Margaret found a note from Ryan shoved through the slats. It was written in eensy teensy print on the back of a candy wrapper in pencil and it said,

> "Margaret . . . meet at my house 22 Ballantine Avenue right after school. Craig is coming. We have to talk. The house is gray."

All day long Margaret waited for the end of school. Every hour was like an eternity and Mrs. Grafton's voice sounded like she was talking through a paper-towel tube.

Late in the afternoon Margaret got her math test back from Mrs. Grafton. It had a gigantic, red D-minus at the top of it. Margaret had taken it the day before during recess as a make-up. The numbers had gotten all jumbled together when she looked at the paper. So she had stared out the window and watched some little girls jumping rope on the black top.

Mrs. Grafton had a hopeless expression on her face as she placed the paper on Margaret's desk. Then she shook her head.

"I know you can do better," she said loud enough for everyone to hear. "We need to go over this."

Margaret's face grew hot but she just shrugged. Heather Fitzgerald, who sat next to Margaret, was staring at her. Heather was Craig's older sister, and she had that same pale blue-eyed stare that he had.

"I don't know why you can't do math, Margaret," Heather whispered as Mrs. Grafton walked away. "This stuff is simple!"

Heather pulled down her hairband, pushed back long, straying strands of light blond hair against her head, and replaced the hairband with dignity. *Heather was just too perfect*, thought Margaret. Everyone liked her, and she knew *everything* about long division. Sometimes Heather was *too* smart, and Mrs. Grafton would have to say, "Heather, let's give some of the rest of the class a chance to answer these questions." Heather would smile sweetly and say, "Of course, Mrs. Grafton."

Then Heather would sigh and take down her hairband. She'd fix her hair, put the band back on, and sit straight and tall in her seat, hands folded and loafers flat on the floor touching one another. Heather's loafers were always shiny with no scratch marks on them. Margaret would trade her own wiry brown braids for that long, silky blond hair any day.

"I think math is stupid," Margaret mumbled. "What did you get on your test?"

"What? The long division test?" Heather sounded surprised. "I got an A, but that was ages ago. I'm already two units beyond the rest of the class and I'm working with Ryan on percentages. He's first in the class in math and I'm second."

"Yeah, well, I got an A on the test before this one," Margaret lied.

"You did not!" Heather retorted condescendingly.

"Did too!"

Margaret didn't talk to Heather for the rest of the afternoon. As far as Margaret was concerned Ryan was a geek from another planet. Who cared about being a whiz at math when you looked like a stalk of asparagus?

Margaret imagined Laurel coming like a big white sheet through the open window and landing right on Mrs. Grafton's desk. Papers would swirl through the air from the force of the swan's wings and all the test tubes lined up along the window ledge would be shattered by the swan's long tail. Mrs. Grafton would fall back against the blackboard and drop her chalk. Everyone would hold their breath. And then Laurel would say in a regal tone,

"I have come to get Margaret Morrison."

Margaret would walk proudly to the front of the room. With long, confident strides she'd pass Mrs. Grafton, climb onto her teacher's desk, and take her place on the back of the enormous swan, settling deeply into its downy fluff. Everyone would be so jealous—even Heather. The swan would open its wide beautiful wings and Mrs. Grafton would gape with amazement as she and Laurel circled once, twice, above the class and then. . . .

"Margaret," came a familiar voice rather icily, "I am speaking to you."

Margaret, who had been looking at the ceiling, jerked upright and faced Mrs. Grafton. The entire class was staring at her.

"Uh, yeah?" Margaret managed.

"Margaret, you are not paying attention!" said her teacher irritably. "You are the last one who can afford to daydream during math class! Now come to the board and do this long division problem."

Margaret stood to her feet stiffly. Making her way to the front, she hesitantly took the chalk that Mrs. Grafton handed to her. The problem was already written out for her in yellow chalk, big and bold on the board. *Mrs. Grafton made her "2's" look like cursive "Q's,"* thought Margaret studying the problem carefully, *and she always crossed her "7's."* Margaret did the problem, but she did it wrong. Mrs. Grafton made her sit down and Heather Fitzgerald went up and did it right. Then the bell rang and the school day was over. Relieved, Margaret gathered her books and headed for the door, but Mrs. Grafton called to her.

Rats! thought Margaret.

"Margaret," began Mrs. Grafton as Margaret slowly approached. Her teacher's light wood desk had construction paper tulips taped all around the sides of it. (Mrs. Grafton liked tulips.)

"Margaret," said Mrs. Grafton again, looking helpless, "you have got to do better in math. You're failing that subject and you are almost failing science as well."

"I'm sorry," said Margaret humbly.

"Sorry isn't enough," said Mrs. Grafton.

Margaret wondered why adults always said that "sorry" wasn't enough.

"I'm going to have to keep you after school until you make some solid improvement in these two subjects. Now sit down. . . ."

"But Mrs. Grafton, I've gotta go . . ." began Margaret.

"Where?" asked her teacher.

"I've got a very important appointment," continued Margaret trying desperately not to lie. She wanted to talk with Craig and Ryan so badly she could scarcely contain herself.

"Is it a doctor's appointment?"

"No," said Margaret, even though she wanted to say "yes."

"Well, then," said her teacher, "what sort of an appointment is it?"

"It's just very important," blundered Margaret.

Mrs. Grafton's eyes were bloodshot. She took off her glasses and rubbed her left eye until Margaret thought her eyeball had popped out of its socket. Then she replaced her glasses with dignity on the tip of her pointy, red nose.

"Margaret . . ." sighed Mrs. Grafton shaking her head, "Margaret. . . ."

"Yes, Mrs. Grafton?"

"Margaret," said Mrs. Grafton suddenly sounding as tired as Uncle John. "I'll let you go, but on Monday you must stay, and I will look for homework from you. Unit twelve—do even numbered problems only, page 345, in pencil. Got it?"

"Got it!" Margaret assured her red-eyed teacher. Then she dashed out of the classroom. She had far more important things to think about than Mrs. Grafton and long division. She was glad Ryan had not spoken to her in school that day. He could have easily taken her aside at any time. *Ryan might be a geek, but he was sensible*, thought Margaret. It would get too complicated if the other kids saw them together. She could just imagine Heather leaning over and asking, "Are you and Ryan going steady? I thought you were enemies!"

Then Margaret would have to think of an explanation. She had ignored Ryan since the first day of school when he had pushed her out of the lunch line. Whatever she said she knew Heather wouldn't believe her anyway, and rumors would begin. It was much easier to meet at Ryan's house than talk in school. Margaret walked rapidly toward Ballantine Avenue. Needless to say, she had never been to Ryan's house before and she had never had the slightest little inkling of a desire to go there. Now she couldn't wait. She was turning a corner when Ryan suddenly emerged from some shrubs by the sidewalk and began walking along next to her.

"It sure took you long enough," he began. "I've been waiting here for ages."

Margaret grimaced.

"That's ridiculous. I left right after school. Why did you wait in a bunch of bushes for me, anyway? I know where I'm going. I got your note. Besides, someone might see us together."

Ryan turned and glanced behind him.

"Naw, there's not a lot of kids in my neighborhood. Nobody's following us. Besides, I was thinking . . . maybe it isn't such a good idea to go to my house."

Margaret stopped walking.

"Why?"

"Well, it's kind of messy. You should see my room. It's got airplane glue all over the carpet and a bunch of clothes on all the chairs. There wouldn't be any place to sit down. Besides, my dog is sick."

Margaret rolled her eyes.

"What's the matter with you?" she demanded. "This was all planned and we can't change now. We'll sit in the kitchen or living room or something. I don't care how messy your house is and your dog won't mind. Besides, I've got to talk to you now!"

"Shhhh," Ryan cautioned. "Not outside. Someone may hear us."

They walked the rest of the way briskly in silence. When they reached the gray house with number 22 on the front door a slight, pleasant-looking woman was in the yard digging in the earth with a trowel. She had on old jeans with holes in the knees and a blue bandanna tied around her head. When Ryan and Margaret came into the yard she brushed her hands together to dust them off. Then she stood to greet them. Although she was a small woman she had a firm handshake, thought Margaret, as she felt her fingers being pressed together in the woman's strong grip of welcome.

"This is my mother," Ryan told Margaret.

"Took the day off to do a little gardening, but it might be a bit early," said the woman with a warm smile at both of them. "Ryan, this must be your little friend you were telling me about."

"This is Margaret," Ryan said in a low voice as if embarrassed.

"Glad to meet you, Margaret. Just call me Wilda."

Margaret noticed that a few feet away from them was someone else digging with a spade in the earth, but the person seemed oblivious to their presence. The figure had on a large straw hat and a blue flannel shirt with yellow lines running through it. The shoulders were broad and masculine, and Margaret thought this person might be Ryan's father.

"Quite a little scrape the two of you were in yesterday," Ryan's mother was saying. "I was quite concerned. Glad to have you just the same. Ryan, aren't you going to introduce Margaret to your brother?"

Ryan gave his mother a shrug.

"Mom, he's busy. Just leave him."

Wilda waved her hand at Ryan in a gesture of frustration. Then she turned to Margaret.

"Margaret, would you like to meet Ryan's brother, Ted?"

"Sure . . . I mean, of course. I didn't even know Ryan had a brother."

Margaret turned to look at Ryan with puzzled curiosity.

"He doesn't go to our school, does he?"

Ryan shook his head and looked down at his feet. Wilda walked over to the figure stooping low over the earth and gave the broad shoulders two light taps. The head under the straw hat looked up for the first time, saw his mother, and then focused beyond her to notice Ryan and Margaret. The boy's face, half-shadowed by the hat, looked flat and white. His nose seemed too wide and his eyes were big, brown, and cavernous with dark rings underneath. When he spied Margaret, however, a loose, open grin spread across his bland expression and he awkwardly got to his feet and came lumbering eagerly over to her. Tentatively he held out a large, meaty hand and Margaret shook it gently. It was moist and thick.

"Teddy loves company," Ryan's mother was saying. "He's always ready to shake hands. That's one of the things he does best."

"I'm pleased to meet you, Teddy," Margaret said looking up at him with awe. He towered over all of them, and had he not been smiling so broadly she would have been a little scared.

"He doesn't talk," Ryan mumbled, still looking down at the ground. "He's slow. You know . . . retarded."

"He knows some sign language," Ryan's mother piped in cheerfully, "and he loves flowers and animals. I think he communicates with them the best. Actually, he was just planting some marigold seeds."

Teddy pulled at Margaret's sleeve making little grunting noises.

"He wants to show you the kitten," Ryan's mother explained. "She's over there in the shed. Teddy found her outside in the rain last night. She was a sight! Looked more like a wet rat than a kitten and ate me out of two bowls of oatmeal."

"Another one?" Ryan moaned. "Gee whiz, Mom! When are you going to make him stop rescuing all these sick animals? They spread disease! Besides, its the weak things that are meant to die off for the good of the rest of us."

"You," said Ryan's mother, pointing a long, skinny finger at him, "will be still. There's no harm in Teddy having his menagerie outside in the shed. It's doing Teddy and the animals a world of good, and I hope you can one day appreciate your brother's efforts."

Ryan rolled his eyes up in his head but said nothing more. Margaret followed Teddy down a little slope in the yard to a white shed that had a small heart-shaped window in one side with blue shutters. Wilda followed closely behind, leaving Ryan to meander reluctantly toward them, head down, hands deep in his pockets. The door was not locked and Teddy simply pushed it open and went in stooping because of his height.

Again Margaret followed him, undaunted by the quiet boy's stature. There was something in his demeanor that made her peaceful and unafraid. She stood blinking in the dim light of the shed for only a few seconds before Teddy placed a light, squirming object in her hands. Looking down she first saw a ball of gray fluff. Then she saw the kitten's tiny dark eyes gleaming at her in the dim light as if they were made of polished marble. Margaret stroked the little creature tenderly and

Teddy looked on adoringly, his mouth open in a wide, steady smile.

Ryan had finally gotten to the shed and stood next to his mother in the open doorway.

"Okay," he demanded after a few moments. "C'mon, Margaret, let's get going."

Reluctantly Margaret handed the kitten back to Teddy, left the shed, and walked up to the house with Ryan.

"You don't much like kittens, do you?" Margaret asked after they'd walked a ways in uncomfortable silence. Ryan still hadn't taken his eyes off the ground. "I think that one was uncommonly cute."

"It's not the kitten, it's my brother. He's a royal pain," Ryan snipped back at her. "Why couldn't I have a normal brother like everybody else? No, I get stuck with him. Everywhere we go people stare at him, and he embarrasses me. He goes through everything I have and messes up my room all the time when I'm not around. He's the one who got airplane glue all over my rug. I'm the one who has to go find him when he wanders. I'm the one who has to clean up after him. I'm the one who gets in trouble if anything goes wrong. He never gets in trouble, and when he does, he doesn't know he's in trouble because he's too stupid to realize it, so it doesn't count. My mom says to be patient because he doesn't know any better. I think he's just trying to irritate me and he does, especially when he takes in all those disease-infested animals. I wish my mom would do something."

"What does your dad do?"

"My dad left us years ago. I was two then and I never saw him again. He probably couldn't take it when my brother was born. At least that's what I think."

"So Teddy's your younger brother?"

"By a year."

"He's gigantic!"

"I know. He's a monster."

"Well," Margaret cleared her throat, "I still think you should be nicer to him. I think it's kind of sweet the way he takes to little hurt creatures like he does."

"You wouldn't think he was sweet if you lived with him," Ryan barked at her, and that was all he would say.

They walked straight ahead into the house and back to the kitchen. Here they found Craig sitting and eating a donut. He had his mouth full but he looked up and waved. Margaret was so glad to see him she almost raced over and hugged him, but she restrained herself.

"How did you get in here?" asked Ryan, absently opening the refrigerator and taking out three cans of soda.

"Thsmwwyusgtnhr," Craig motioned with a full mouth blowing white donut powder in the air.

"Gross!" said Margaret. "Finish chewing."

"The same way I usually get in here," tried Craig again after he swallowed. "Through the door. Ha!"

Ryan and Margaret sat down around the kitchen table and neither of them laughed.

"My mother gave me all these donuts for everyone," Craig continued undaunted, dumping a brown paper sack filled with powdered donuts onto the middle of the table. "They're a day old, but my dad says that we might have to start selling these too if things don't get better, so enjoy them now."

"You could have used a plate," suggested Margaret.

"Now," said Ryan, "I guess we can begin."

He got up, opened a drawer, and took out a wooden

spoon, which he pounded three times on the kitchen table for silence. Then he sat down again.

"Well," said Ryan after a moment's pause when he grabbed a donut. "Well, we're all here because we all saw something and heard something that no one else would believe."

"What's that?" asked Craig.

"The swan, dummy!" Ryan exclaimed, exasperated.

"Boy, are you ever in a bad mood," Craig whined. "Why won't anyone believe us that we saw a swan?"

"You saw it too, Ryan? Honest?" Margaret cried leaning forward across the table and looking him in the eye.

Ryan nodded vigorously. Margaret felt tingles rushing down her spine.

"It's not just that we saw a swan, Craig," she continued elated. "The swan talked to us. He told us his name and he saved your life. Didn't he, Ryan?"

Ryan nodded again and looked very serious.

"It did?" asked Craig.

"Don't you remember anything, Craig?" asked Margaret, dumbfounded.

Craig shook his head.

"I did have this dream that I was flying," Craig mumbled into his donut. "Before I woke up on the river bank."

"Flying where?" Ryan demanded.

Craig thought for a minute.

"Over things," he said finally. "Just over things."

"The swan," said Ryan slowly, "only spoke to you and me, Margaret. We're the only ones who heard Laurel speak."

"All day that's all I've been thinking about," Margaret whispered excitedly. "Whether or not I really knew a talking swan. Ryan, it wasn't just a dream was it? You saw it too, didn't you?"

She had to ask him again to be absolutely positive. That's the only way you could test impossibility.

Ryan nodded.

"I was there," he said seriously enough to be an adult. "No one will ever be able to tell me otherwise. We saw a swan and he talked to us."

Margaret let out a sigh. She was convinced.

"What did the swan say?" asked Craig.

"Never mind," said Margaret. "I'll tell you later."

"I went to the river," began Ryan clearing his throat, "early this morning before school."

He looked at Margaret soberly.

"I think Laurel needs our help, Margaret."

"Me too?" asked Craig blowing powder in the air again. "Can I help too?"

"So," said Margaret impatiently, ignoring Craig. "What happened when you went to the river?"

Ryan looked at Craig.

"Don't interrupt!" he ordered, pounding the spoon on the table. "And if you tell a soul about what I'm going to say, I'll never speak to you again!"

Craig slumped in his chair and began to pout.

"I went to the river," Ryan began again softly. "I was sort of walking around it wondering if what I had seen yesterday had only been a dream when I smelled that smell—you know the one Margaret—some kind of flower and pine needles or something. It was so strong, and then I heard this music, down by the river. I can't explain what it sounded like. It was something I'd never heard before and it just drew me. Like maybe harp music mixed with falling water or something. It was like I couldn't get enough of it."

Ryan paused and ran his fingers through his hair until it stuck up straighter than straight.

"Go on!" Margaret pumped eagerly. "Then what?"

"You interrupted," said Craig, "so why can't I interrupt? I have a question."

"Because you're only eight years old," retorted Margaret annoyed. "Go on Ryan."

"Well, I walked down closer to the river where we had seen the swan before, and sitting there in the sunlight pruning his feathers was . . . well, you know."

"Are you sure?"

"You interrupted again," said Craig to Margaret. "That's twice you've interrupted."

"Be quiet!" said Ryan banging the table with his palm forgetting momentarily about his spoon. "Both of you! Or I won't tell you anything!"

"Go on," said Margaret.

Ryan took a deep breath and continued.

"So Laurel is sitting there in the sunlight looking mighty handsome. That swan is whiter in the sunlight than anything I can think of. He's white like a pearl is white, or like snow when it first falls. Anyway, he turns, looks at me and smiles, and says, 'Greetings!' and I didn't quite know why I was so glad to see him, but I was. I mean, I was ecstatic. It's like you wish more than anything that you were a swan yourself when you see him. All this color was flashing around him in the water and it was so bright and it was dancing so much that I could hardly see at first. Gradually I got used to it and then he says, 'Ryan!' That's all he said was just 'Ryan!' but when he said it, tingly vibes went through me and I didn't answer at first. I wasn't sure I wanted to answer because I knew that if I did I would have to listen to what he said next. I had this funny feeling he was going to tell me something that I had to do, and I wasn't sure I wanted to do it. And all the time he's looking at me with dark, deep eyes that sparkled and danced and drew me into them. How do you not answer someone like that? So finally I draw in my breath, prepare for the worst, and barely say the word, 'What?' And right away he says to me. . . ."

Ryan paused and ran his fingers through his hair again.

"Go on!" said Margaret, nearly jumping out of her seat. "Tell us what he said!"

"He said," Ryan began again and cleared his throat. "He said, 'I only have a short time here, Ryan, and I need your help. Will you help me make a way to Joona?' "

There was a pause.

"Go on!" demanded Margaret. "What does that mean, anyway?"

"That's three times you've interrupted," Craig told her.

"Well, that's just what I asked," said Ryan shaking his head. "I'm still not sure I understand it. When I asked what he wanted me to do, Laurel just fluffed up his feathers and said, 'Come back with your friends, Ryan, and call my name. Two or three together is the mystery of the way things are.' Then, right when Laurel was speaking, there was a kind of roar and a mighty flash of color. I hid my eyes and when I looked there was nothing but a slight bit of pink color in the water where he'd just been floating."

"That's dumb," said Craig biting deeply into his fourth powdered donut. "You must have been drunk or something."

Both Margaret and Ryan looked startled. They looked at each other and then at Craig dumbfounded.

"He saved your life and you don't believe in him?" Ryan asked incredulously. "Why, that's just plain rude."

Craig started to whine.

"Well how do *I* know? *I* didn't see him. And swans don't talk!"

"Laurel does," stated Margaret simply. "That's just the way it is."

Craig shrugged.

"Forget him," counseled Ryan to Margaret with a wave of his hand. "He's just immature."

"What's that? What's immachoor?" Craig insisted.

"It's when you don't believe in things that are, just because they don't fit what you think is possible," explained Margaret obligingly after a moment's thought.

"That doesn't make any sense," retorted Craig stubbornly. "I think you are both dumb."

"Now what?" Margaret asked. "When do we see Laurel again?"

"I'm not sure what to do," Ryan said. "I didn't get a chance to ask. I do know there's something very important in store for us. I feel it all over me."

"Obviously, all of us have to go to the river," Margaret stated matter of factly. "Then we've got to find the swan and get more information."

"Laurel wants us all there," Ryan agreed.

"I'm grounded," sighed Margaret. "But if we could meet by the bridge, real early in the morning, like about six o'clock, I could leave and get back before Uncle John even wakes up. I'm great at sneaking around that old house."

"Six o'clock?!" moaned Craig. "No one gets up at six o'clock! My dad doesn't even milk the cows until six-thirty!"

"That's what makes it a good time," Ryan said fiercely, glaring at Craig.

"I can't believe you two hang together," Margaret retorted. "But," she continued grabbing her book bag, "I've got to get going. I've stayed too long already, and now I've got to run all the way home."

4
THE STORY OF JOONA

Margaret's alarm did not go off the next morning, and she would have slept in had not a woodpecker tapped a resounding "rat-a-tat-tat" on her window to see if the glass were edible. She jolted awake and saw that it was several minutes after six o'clock. Jerking on her overalls, she sped out the door barefoot. The morning air was misty and the grass was wet and warm against her feet. When she finally reached the swinging bridge she was out of breath. Ryan was already there with Craig. They were sitting on the bridge with their legs dangling over the side looking down into the river.

"It's about time," snorted Craig when he saw Margaret appear on the bank. "This was your idea and you're late."

"We've been waiting for you," said Ryan impatiently. "Let's call him."

"Wait," said Margaret. She climbed the cement steps to the bridge and settled herself down next to Craig.

"We'll all call," she said. "One, two, three!"

"Laurel!"

The leaves whispered to each other in a light breeze that made the ripples in the water wrinkle toward them. The fragrance of lilac came and went through Margaret's nostrils. The daffodils bowed to her from the edge of the bank where they grew, and the sun, hazy in the early dawn, touched the water with flecks of golden light. At first there was nothing. Then Ryan saw Laurel coming and he pointed. The swan emerged from around the bend in the river swimming effortlessly toward them upstream.

"It worked!" Ryan said softly.

Margaret held her breath. Laurel's neck arched regally, but as he approached the children his neck bent down low in a swan smile.

Margaret scrambled off the bridge, jumped into the water, and began swimming toward the swan. Ryan followed her, but before they could swim very far at all the swan was suddenly with them, nosing them around in the water with his bill and flapping his wings delightedly. Margaret grabbed the base of the swan's neck and held onto it. Laurel sank and rose underneath her and Margaret found herself seated on the swan's back. She held onto his slender neck and pressed her wet face up against his bony cheek. Ryan was also scooped up onto Laurel's broad back and the two of them petted the enormous bird wordlessly.

Craig stood dumbfounded on the bank staring at them, interlocking and undoing his fingers again and again.

"Greetings!" Laurel said to Craig, paddling over to him with Ryan and Margaret astride his back. "I suppose you figure you've had your ride already."

"It talks!" Craig gasped, jumping back a few inches. His eyes got rounder and rounder.

"That it does!" Laurel declared pleasantly. "Haven't you ever heard the phrase, 'Birds of a feather talk together'?"

"I think it's *flock*," said Ryan.

"That came later," Laurel said. "Actually, quite later after they all forgot how—to talk, that is. That's when they decided to flock instead."

"Oh," said Ryan.

"So talk we shall!" Laurel declared. "I have scads of things to tell you and I can't wait a moment longer. Shall we go on land?"

Ryan and Margaret slipped back into the water and waded up the moist, muddy bank. Laurel climbed after them. The swan seemed so much more awkward on land than in the water, thought Margaret. They climbed the embankment and Laurel followed, flapping occasionally for balance. There were three moss-covered stumps from pine trees waiting for them at the top. One stood near a lilac bush not quite in bloom, though Margaret could see tight little buds beginning to form at the base of the branches. She decided to sit there.

The swan settled down on a cushion of brown pine needles and looked each of them over carefully.

"How would you define a secret, children?" the swan asked suddenly.

"Something that you're not supposed to tell anyone," Ryan said.

"Quite true," pondered Laurel for a moment. "And if you told someone a secret it would change what was a secret to a nonsecret. Don't you agree?"

Ryan nodded.

"It is quite the same with me, children. You might say, I suppose, that once a secret stops being a secret it loses all its magic that makes it what it is. And were you to tell someone about me, I too would lose my magic. Do you catch my drift, Ryan?"

Ryan nodded again adamantly.

"We won't tell a soul," he said with resolve. "No one would believe us anyway."

"I already told someone," Margaret said softly. She reached down to the ground, picked up a leaf, and began ripping it into shreds.

"You what?" Ryan gawked at her in disbelief.

"I'm sorry," Margaret said. "I didn't know what else to do."

"Who did you tell?" asked the swan gently.

"My Uncle John. He made me tell."

The swan seemed amused at this and shook his tail feathers lightly as if chuckling.

"Don't worry, Margaret," Laurel said sticking his neck toward her and speaking softly. "Your uncle is quite an exception. He is already in on the secret, although as an adult he most probably doubts, as most of them do, which is why I never use adults. They find it hard to believe in the reality of impossibility, if you catch my drift. It was he and your mother who met me here, in this very place, twenty years ago.

Margaret couldn't believe her ears.

"You knew my mother?" she gasped.

"Yes dear," Laurel said nodding vigorously. "She is now queen of the swans."

"She died," Margaret said lowly, throwing her shredded leaf to the wind. "She's nothing now."

The swan looked at her surprised.

"She may have died, Margaret," Laurel said with sudden firmness. "But to say that she's nothing now is a lie. It's simply not true, if you want to say it another way. Or you might say it's absolutely impossible for something that is to become something that isn't. It's quite awkward for me to even start thinking that way, so if you don't mind, I won't. I told you, Margaret. Your mother is queen of the swans."

Margaret hung on every word Laurel said. It was as if she had always known that her mother hadn't just disappeared into nothingness. But something insidious inside her head had told her she was silly to believe it was so. She had been thinking like an adult, and it rather scared her.

"What do you mean?" Margaret asked softly. "What do you mean, my mother is queen of the swans?"

"Precisely what I said, dear," Laurel retorted. "Any person who has done something kind for a swan at one time or another in their lifetime, why, the gates of Joona are open wide to them when it is time for them to journey from this earth. People who are kind to swans find Joona to be a paradise, and nearly everyone stays on there."

"Will you take me to her?" Margaret pleaded. "To that place—what did you call it? Jeenoo?"

"Joona," corrected the swan. "I might be able to take you to see her, but I couldn't land. Once I landed you'd never be able to return to earth again, and your time hasn't come yet."

Margaret jumped up.

"I wouldn't care!" she exclaimed. "No, I wouldn't care at all! To see her, one more time. That's all I want. Please, Laurel, please! Please take me to Joona!"

The swan eyed Margaret with compassion.

"You know I would, Margaret. I would do it this instant if I could. But I can't do it now—at least not yet. A terrible thing has happened, children. The dark swan has blocked the passageway to Joona and the rainbow's light is fading."

Ryan looked at Margaret and scowled. Craig stared blankly ahead of him. None of them understood what Laurel was talking about. The swan rearranged himself on the bed of pine needles and snorted.

"Children," Laurel continued, "let me tell you about Joona."

Margaret sat down cross-legged close to the swan. Ryan and Craig settled back to listen.

"Now then," began Laurel. He took a deep breath and began.

"Before time even came to be with us, children, Joona has been a place where suffering swans go when they have had all that they can take of this life and are ready for something better. Every so often I come to gather all the suffering swans who will follow me and I take them back to Joona. I have always been chief messenger of Joona. It is impossible for the suffering swans to find the passageway from earth to Joona on their own unless they allow me to lead them to it. Actually, children, you cannot imagine how perfectly cynical and suspicious most swans are. It is very hard convincing them to believe that Joona was made just for them. Many of them won't come back with me because they refuse to accept that joy is still possible for them.

"Joona was made for joy, children—only for joy and nothing else. It is mostly made up of sparkling water with one large glistening rainbow shining in the sky. The rainbow watches over the land and often will sing songs to the swans as they dive through the colorful bows of light and echo back the rainbow's melody. The swans that live in Joona are so happy and well-fed that they are always slightly plump. They grow sleek, long feathers that feel like satin. Swans grow to huge sizes in Joona and have great strength. Each time I bring in a new band of suffering swans the rainbow cheers and grows brighter. Joona thrives and lives because it is open to any swan who might be suffering, and the land cannot continue to exist unless it is shared. Which brings me to the point."

The swan paused and cleared his throat.

"There is only one swan who ever went to Joona and found it unsatisfactory. His name is Sebastian, but he is known throughout Joona as the 'dark swan.' Sebastian was hit by an automobile. I found him lame and starving at the side of the road. He readily agreed to follow me to Joona. What choice did he have? For a while Sebastian seemed quite happy in Joona. In fact, he could not believe that everything was so much to his liking. I remember him thanking me for bringing him to such a wonderful place where the waters teemed with his favorite seaweed. It was only after the next few batches of suffering swans arrived that Sebastian started to become very upset. He felt that the waters would soon be too crowded, that because swans never die in Joona the area would become terribly congested after a time. He wanted to close off Joona to any more suffering swans. I remember when he approached me. Because I am Joona's chief messenger I am easily accessible (when not on assignment) on the floating island that sits in the middle of the waters. It is a beautiful island filled with lilac bushes and pine trees. The swans always know where they can find me. I am under a certain lilac bush by the edge of the water always ready to talk to any swan who has a question or concern. I welcome visits gladly. However, when Sebastian arrived I shuddered. I had never seen a swan in Joona look so upset before.

"'We must do something,' he told me with deep furrows in his feathered brow and a sour expression around the corners of his beak, 'about all these newcomers. It isn't right that they should have access to this land at any moment, at any time. Those of us who have been here longer should preserve the unspoiled, uncrowded atmosphere that Joona has always enjoyed.'

"When he said this, I laughed. I think I might have hurt his feelings, but I could not fathom how anyone could think they could enjoy something more by forcing others to enjoy it less. The whole idea was so preposterous that I think I half hoped Sebastian was kidding. He was not. I tried to explain to him that the only way the rainbow would continue to shine, and the only way his favorite seaweed would stay alive in the water, was if Joona continued to be shared with many swans for eons and eons throughout eternity. I told him that was the nature of the way things were. Joona was a land, as beautiful as it was, precisely because it was shared and open to anyone who would come. It had far more room than he had any idea, and without new swans entering in, he could be assured that the rainbow would stop shining. In fact, I told him that I actually planned my visits to earth by determining the brightness of the rainbow. Whenever I see the rainbow's colors growing dimmer and the deeper pools in the shining water growing darker, I know the rainbow is feeling the pain of all suffering swans on earth and longs to relieve it. It is then that I know I must go to earth and gather more of the suffering swans and bring them back to Joona.

"Each time I arrive with them, the rainbow is ecstatic and bursts forth with flashes of light. It continues to shine in full brilliance for a long, long time. I told Sebastian all of this, slowly and carefully, repeating myself several times, but it did not please him. He was very disagreeable and even spat at the ground a couple of times and waddled about quite perturbed. Finally, he left looking mad. I never saw Sebastian again. Rumor had it that he had left the area. I found out later that he had reentered the passageway—the tunnel by which all swans make their way from earth to Joona. He had taken up residence there and was planning to prevent anyone from passing through. He learned evil magic in the darkness of the tunnel from the reptile creatures that lived in the crannies of the rocks. He dammed up the flow of water that ran through the tunnel so that instead of swimming to Joona's river, the suffering swans had to walk a long distance on dry, crusty sand before arriving at the river that would bring them to Joona. I was convinced Sebastian's jealousy would be short-lived, and I led many suffering swans to the river on foot. Each time, when I opened the stone door to the cave's passageway from earth's side, I kept hoping that the river would gush out to meet us. But children! This time it was far worse than anything I had ever imagined!"

The swan sighed and appeared completely at a loss for words. He shook his head back and forth very slowly three times.

"What was worse than you imagined?" asked Craig.

Laurel rolled his eyes emphatically and looked from one child to the next as he spoke.

"The rainbow was growing dim again and I knew I needed to come to earth. So I entered the tunnel and swam as far as I could on the river until it turned to dry, crusty sand. I made a left turn, the usual way to earth, and I had gone only a couple hundred yards when I heard a loud rushing sound. I looked back to see what was happening and I saw a large wave hurtling toward me through the tunnel. It was ugly green, slimy water filled with dirt and debris. I was sure it would knock me over, but the wave never got to me. It receded a few feet behind me. When it did however, it left a wall of dirt, roots, rocks, sludge, and seaweed so big that it completely blocked the passageway.

"It is the magic of the dark swan, children. The passageway to Joona is now blocked and neither I nor the suffering swans can get through. I have been here on earth far too long already. I know that if I don't get back to Joona quickly, the rainbow will fade and Joona will be in darkness. And if the rainbow fades completely, children, there can be no life in Joona ever again."

A breeze came up and blew Margaret's hair around her face. Ryan leaned forward as if he were about to say something but didn't. Craig sat motionless, his pale blue eyes fixed on Laurel. It was clear that the swan had finished and was now looking each of them over carefully.

"What can we do?" Margaret asked quietly after a long pause. "Please tell us."

She did not want the beautiful rainbow to fade or the suffering swans to continue suffering. Even more compelling was the longing she saw in Laurel's eyes and the thought that she might see her mother again.

"Yeah, I don't get it," Ryan blurted out. "What can we do? We're not swans."

"What a pity," said Laurel matter of factly, "Although as human children you have something that I certainly don't have."

"And what is that?" Ryan asked.

"You are landbred creatures, made for the earth. Made to work on the land. You are not clumsy on earth as we are. You don't, shall I say," and here Laurel lowered his voice, "*waddle*." Laurel said the word *waddle* as if it were some kind of forbidden curse word. Then he continued.

"You children have arms and hands and strength in your legs. I need your strength to clear the passageway for the suffering swans, but it must all be done at night so that it remains a secret."

"Sounds impossible!" Craig pronounced wiping his nose on his sleeve.

"We'll do it," Margaret declared glancing at Ryan to see if he were with her. Ryan glanced back at her and nodded slightly.

"Children," cautioned the swan with concern, "I should tell you there is much darkness in the tunnel. Clearing the passageway will make Sebastian very angry. It will undo his evil magic and put you at his mercy."

"Forget it!" broke in Craig loudly. "There's no way I can handle this."

"Be quiet, Craig!" Ryan ordered. "No one asked for your opinion. Laurel, do you think we have a chance, I mean, against the dark swan's magic?"

"You mustn't ever be afraid or take yourselves too seriously," the swan instructed slowly, looking each of them in the eyes, one by one. "You must remember that I will always be with you, even if you can't see me. You must remember that the magic of the dark swan is camouflage and lies. If you remember these things you will find yourselves successful. Becoming involved in this mission must be your choice. It must be something you want to do, not something you must do. Otherwise the mission will fail."

"When do we get started?" Margaret asked.

"Tonight, after midnight, when you call me I will meet you. It will be rather exciting, actually, don't you think?"

"Perhaps," said Ryan uncertainly. "I'll be ready, Laurel."

Craig looked disappointed at Ryan's response. The swan looked at Craig steadily waiting for his answer. So did Ryan and Margaret. Finally he shrugged.

"I'll try," he stated flatly. "I'll come tonight anyway."

"So be it," the swan agreed. "Children, you must be very careful not to let anyone know where we are going. Oh yes, I nearly forgot. Come here Margaret . . . come close."

Margaret stood up and took a step forward.

"Now, under my wing," the swan continued stretching out his wing to its full expanse. "Look underneath."

Margaret crouched down and looked.

"Do you see a feather that is speckled, Margaret? Speckled, perhaps brown and black, where all the rest are white?"

Margaret spotted it at once.

"Yes," she said.

"Pull it out!"

Margaret hesitated.

"Won't it hurt you?"

"Go on dear. Pull it out."

Margaret took the spotted feather in her hands and pulled. Ryan saw the swan wince.

"It's not coming out," she told the swan apologetically. "I'm sorry if I hurt you."

"Try again," Laurel ordered.

Margaret took the feather and, this time, with a deliberate yank, she plucked it from the swan's body.

"I've got it," she announced. "I'm sorry if I hurt you."

Laurel blinked back tears.

"It's quite all right," the swan said, talking rapidly as if to subdue the pain. "I have just given you something very valuable, children. A feather that is not for fair weather you might say."

For a moment Laurel was mildly amused at the rhyme but then grew serious again.

"I want you to keep that feather for this mission and never let it out of your possession. It will counter the magic of the dark swan. When you use it, hold it out in front of you and say my name over and over."

Margaret looked at the spotted feather. It was long and sleek but otherwise quite ordinary. She tucked it into her front bib pocket. The swan spread his wings and flapped the aromatic scent of pine and lilac into the children's faces. Then it looked upward at the sky.

"I don't know how to thank you, children. You have brought a great deal of joy to me today and I feel the need to fly." Laurel bent down low in a swan smile. "I need to be close to the sky for a while. I can't stay grounded for long, you see. It makes everything seem so very commonplace and small. You will understand what I mean tonight, children. After midnight I will see you. Call me!"

The three of them stood and watched Laurel spread white wings to the morning sky and effortlessly float into the hazy morning air. The swan circled above them twice and then with a stately farewell vanished into the fleecy mist that rested like shredded cotton on the face of the water.

5
THE NIGHT FLIGHT

It must have been 12:30 a.m. that morning when Margaret was awakened by a bumping at her window. She sat bolt upright in bed, and for a moment she was too afraid to move. The window was facing her, and the hall light refracting against the pane caused an eerie glare. Still, she could see a white object bobbing up and down outside in front of the glass occasionally banging into it. She couldn't make out what it was, but she threw back the covers and tiptoed quietly to the window. Her room was on the second floor. Looking down, at first she could see nothing. The porch light was on, but after blinking a few times she saw a dark, gangly silhouette she immediately recognized as Ryan. Then she remembered. This was the night they were to begin their mission and once again her faulty alarm had made her late. Ryan was holding his hightop in one hand but obviously didn't see her peering down at him for he was aiming to throw it again. Margaret yanked up the window and it made a dreadfully loud screech. She waited tensely for a step in the hall but none came. All was quiet.

"Gee whiz, you sure do sleep like you're dead," Ryan

yelled up, too loudly, of course. "I've been out here forever."

Margaret put her finger to her lips.

"Shhhh!" she rasped in a loud whisper. "My alarm is broken."

"I knew that this morning!" Ryan began too loudly again. "Hurry up!"

"Be quiet!" hissed Margaret who was convinced this gangly silhouette would wake up the whole neighborhood. "I'm coming down right now."

Margaret backed away from the window soundlessly. Swiftly she pulled her overalls (which were still slightly damp from the morning's swim) on over her pajamas and pushed the door of her bedroom all the way open. She was grateful that John always left the hall light on. Tiptoeing to the staircase, she let herself down one step at a time. Margaret knew Auntie Emily had ears that could hear miles and miles away. Nonetheless, she was confident. She had gone down this staircase many times and knew just where to place her foot on the splintered wooden steps to make the least amount of noise. When she finally got to the bottom step she had made only four creaks, and they had been small ones. It was a record breaker! Her sweater was hanging on the doorknob of the closet. She pulled it on and unlocked the back door. Opening it ever so slightly she squeezed out into the cool night air. Ryan was standing in the shadows against the wall under the guest room window where Auntie Emily was probably sleeping.

"Gee whiz, Margaret!" Ryan exclaimed too loudly again.

"*Shhhh!*" Margaret grabbed his arm and dragged him a good distance away from the house until they stood in a little clearing toward the back of the yard surrounded by pine trees. The moon was bright and the crickets were singing faintly, far away. When the breeze blew, Margaret could smell the fragrance of the pine trees whispering together in the cool of the night air.

"Okay now!" Margaret said quietly clasping her hands together, "Let's call him."

"On three," said Ryan. "One . . . two . . . three."

They had to yell it in a loud whisper, and for a fleeting instant Margaret feared the swan would not hear them.

"You called?" a regal voice sounded from behind them. Both children swung around quickly but could see nothing. The breeze gusted their faces and Margaret was suddenly aware that the fragrance of lilac was now mixing gently with the scent of pine.

"It's Laurel," she whispered to Ryan. She felt her heartbeat increase as she gazed intently into the blackness.

"It's really a lovely night to be out!" said the voice growing closer. There was a rustling of leaves and Laurel emerged into the clearing. The swan bowed its long neck low in greeting and the white feathers on its back glistened silver in the moonlight. It was clear to the children that Laurel was smiling.

"Greetings! I am glad you called according to plan," the swan continued with a hint of excitement in his voice. "The river is beautiful at night and the sky glorious."

"I didn't know if you could hear us," Margaret said. "We called so softly I wasn't sure."

"You had faith I would hear you or you wouldn't have called at all," piped Laurel happily. "And here we are!"

"I suppose," said Ryan, "that we should get to work."

"Yes, yes, by all means!" prattled the swan sweetly,

"But not before we have a bit of play as well. The sky is just too beautiful tonight to miss. I want to share it with you."

"What do you want us to do, Laurel?" Margaret asked curiously, "I can't go far . . . I'm grounded."

"What a pity," the swan declared frankly. "Although most humans are, aren't they? No wings."

Margaret smiled.

"It's very simple," Laurel continued. "With my wings you'll be 'ungrounded,' and everything will look so different from the sky."

"I don't understand," Margaret said warily.

"I'm afraid of heights," Ryan confessed.

"Nonsense!" Laurel laughed an endearing laugh that sounded like someone had run their fingers over the strings of a harp. "You're not afraid of heights, Ryan. You're afraid of falling down from them! Don't fear, my child. That will never happen when you are with me."

"Even that swinging bridge made me sick and woozy," Ryan continued emphatically.

"It did?" asked Margaret incredulously, "You seemed so unafraid and daring."

"Things are rarely what they seem," said the swan. "Children!" Laurel continued with a sudden urgency. "Climb on my back and see the world a different way!"

"On your back?" gasped Ryan.

Out of the corner of her eye Margaret saw a light go on in the living room window. Then she heard the sound of the brass lock on the back door being turned. The swan was bending low against the moonlit moss and pine needles, wings outstretched, waiting for their mount.

"Children!" cried Laurel again, "Hurry, or I shall have to leave without you."

The front door swung open with a loud groan, and the light from the living room flooded the lawn. Margaret saw the stout figure of Auntie Emily in the door frame peering out into the night. The sight of her Aunt spurred Margaret to action. Grabbing Ryan's arm, she half-dragged, half-pushed him toward the swan. Laurel was so large that when they reached the swan's side it was clear that to get up on the bird's broad, silvery back it was necessary to scramble up Laurel's wing. This was not a simple task, for the wing was sleek and slippery and touched the ground on an angle. It was like trying to climb a ramp with no foothold. Nor was Ryan particularly agile or thrilled by the prospect of riding a swan.

"I can't do this, Margaret," he said slipping and falling backwards down three-fourths of the wing on his second try.

Margaret saw Auntie Emily click on a flashlight and walk toward the porch steps.

"She's coming over here and she'll kill us if she finds us," Margaret stammered. "We've got no choice."

"Hurry, children!" commanded the swan bending down lower, "You've only a few seconds left before I must leave."

Margaret pushed Ryan out of the way and began inching her way up the wing on her hands and knees. Ryan followed suit behind her. It seemed an eternity, but it was only moments before Margaret tumbled onto the broad silvery surface of the bird's back. Leaning way over, she reached out and just managed to grab Ryan's outstretched hand enough to drag him up beside her. She could see Auntie Emily, now scanning the yard meticulously with the flashlight, growing closer every moment. Yet she was no longer afraid. Laurel shuddered briefly. As he did so, the mammoth feathers on his back shuffled up completely around them and held Ryan and Margaret comfortably in place. Then came a thunderous noise as the swan began to flap his enormous wings. Ryan and Margaret covered their ears. Auntie Emily looked at the sky and ran for shelter. The next day folks downtown talked about the thunderstorm with no rain. If Margaret or Ryan had been able to listen carefully to the noise, they would have found it distinct from the thunder of a rainstorm. The swan's flapping sounded more like the clapping of an audience after a stunning performance, except that this clapping was rhythmic and much louder. Tiny fluffy feathers blew up into the night air from the swan's wings and then rocked themselves gently to the ground below. Margaret's eyes followed one of them as it whirled upward and then floated down, down, down. As she watched the feather land, she suddenly realized she was watching it from a great distance and that she and Ryan were already airborne.

It was not at all as scary as she had thought it might be. Definitely not as scary as Auntie Emily in her nightgown with her flashlight searching for them in the backyard. The lights of the town grew smaller and smaller as the swan continued to ascend until looking down was the same as looking up at the night sky. Hundreds of twinkling lights shone below them and hundreds above them.

All Margaret could think about was how quickly everything had changed—how small the town had become! Everyone always said Rowley was a small town, but Margaret never realized how small. It was just one little colony of lights in the midst of other colonies of lights, as far as the eye could see, nestled in hills beyond hills beyond hills which, at night, were no more than dusty shadows against the dark horizon. Mrs. Grafton had said once that people could only be in one place at one time, but at this moment Margaret wasn't quite sure. She could see the *whole town* of Rowley, all at once, plus all the other towns beyond. She could certainly feel a whole lot all at one time also. She could feel the breeze of the night air against her skin and the warm down of the swan's feathers against her legs. She could look up and almost touch the radiant, sugary texture of the stars, and she could see the face of the man on the moon looking at her as if he were real. That was pretty close to being in more than one place at one time, probably the closest she would ever be. The swan leveled off and banked gently to the right. Everything was still and silent. There was no noise except the rhythmic flapping of the swan's wings as they pummeled the atmosphere.

"Awesome," Margaret whispered to herself.

Glancing over at Ryan, she saw that he was sitting all doubled up and was covering his ears with his hands. His eyes were wrinkled shut and he looked pale. She reached over and tapped his shoulder but there was no response.

"We're up!" shouted Margaret prying his hand away from his ear. "Look at us, Ryan! We're flying!"

"I can't look," he gasped.

"Don't be scared or you'll miss everything!" persisted Margaret, "Look up if you're afraid to look down. The stars are so close!"

Timidly, Ryan lifted his head and looked up at the stars. Then he looked at Margaret, then he took his hands away from his ears.

"It's not so noisy anymore," he said shakily.

"It hasn't been noisy for a while. That was just takeoff. Look around! You're missing everything!"

"I should be home in bed," said Ryan, looking back up at the stars. "I wonder how many there are."

"Stars?"

"Yeah, stars. How many do you suppose there are?"

"More than you could ever count," said Margaret gazing at the studded heavens.

"I think I'll look down now," Ryan decided after he successfully found the big dipper and proudly showed Margaret. "I probably shouldn't miss this."

"Once you look up I think it's easier to look down," Margaret encouraged. "It looks the same on the ground as it does when you look at the stars."

Ryan braced himself and peered down over the swan's shoulder. He didn't say anything for a long while.

"There's tons of lights," he finally reported calmly, "and they're all in little clumps all over the place."

"I know," said Margaret. "I can't believe we actually live down there inside one of those lights."

"It's incredibly quiet," Ryan said again, as if he hadn't heard. "I mean, I've been in airplanes before, but there's always that rumbling of the engine and the stewardess at the front telling you how to breathe normally into that orange mask. Then sometimes there are movies on the longer flights, people talking, and babies crying. You hardly even know you're in the air, and it's so noisy. Here it's still and mysterious."

"Maybe they make planes like that because people get scared when their houses and land look too small from the sky," suggested Margaret. "Maybe that's why they watch a movie and make a lot of noise."

"Could be," shrugged Ryan. "Things do look awful different from up here. Where are we going, anyway?"

"To the tunnel in the mountain," the swan shouted back over his left shoulder. "Please excuse my silence for the past few minutes, children. It's a bit more taxing taking two or three of you flying than simply swimming one of you upriver."

"Let's go the long way," suggested Ryan eagerly. "I want to see the sights!"

"I'm glad to see you've overcome your fear of falling down from heights," Laurel chuckled. "So let's ride the currents down, my friend. What do you say?"

Before Ryan had a chance to answer, the swan stopped flapping and hung motionless for a split second. Ryan was just about to suggest that perhaps riding the currents wasn't the greatest idea when the swan called out, "This is the fun part!" and spiraled downward, wings spread wide. The children were locked in place by the bird's feathers and could not flail about. The only thing they were aware of were the lights beneath them growing closer and closer and spinning around and around like a top.

Then there was a sudden drop, as there often is when you ride a roller coaster and there's a dip in the track and your stomach gets stuck in your chest. It was as if an invisible cord holding them up in space had been cut, and they fell without warning straight down toward the earth. Margaret's braids blew out behind her and she screamed. Ryan sat paralyzed with his small, brown eyes bulging out of their sockets. Then, almost as quickly as they had plummeted, they were caught again and effortlessly lifted up and up and over, and they soared back up into the night air. Laurel's wings remained motionless as they banked and dipped and were carried high and low again on the gentle currents of the wind. Margaret, who had been certain she was plummeting to her death, jabbed Ryan in the ribs with her elbow and began to smile. Ryan shivered and continued to stare straight ahead. Margaret thought his eyes looked like the eyes of her pet guppy.

"Here we go one more time," piped the swan merrily, "Ready or not!"

Again Laurel spiraled and plummeted and was caught tenderly by the wind. The swan rose and fell and rose again as if it were dancing a waltz in the sky with the invisible forces of the night air. There were no jerks or jolts. The movements of the swan through the sky were smooth and flowing like a signature being signed with a paintbrush. Margaret felt exhilarated.

"One more time, Laurel, please!" she begged.

"It is fun, isn't it?" agreed the swan. "All right, once more."

Ryan looked at Margaret as if he were ready to kill. For over an hour they played in the sky, promising themselves that each ride would be their last one. Even Ryan became more accustomed to the plummeting and cheered up a bit toward the end.

"We must stop," said the swan with sudden resolve after a daring plummet that left the children breathless. "We must get along to the mountain."

They leveled off and began to fly rapidly. They were low in the sky now, barely higher than the tips of the dark pines they cruised by. Soon a silver serpentine river appeared far below them. Margaret could see the dark outlines of the pines in its surface and the glint of moonlight on the ripples.

"I know where we are," declared Ryan. "The swinging bridge is just around this bend."

"You know the river well," Laurel affirmed.

They now began to follow the circuitous route of the river, descending below the pines and flying only about eight feet above the water. It was cooler near the water, and Margaret settled herself deeper into the downy fluff. Around the bend, as Ryan had predicted, suspended in mid-air like a welcoming smile, was the bridge. It looked like it was holding the river together purposefully, as if it thought its absence would cause the two dark banks to drift farther and farther apart. Then, no bridge, however long, would ever be able to connect the distant sides. The bridge creaked slightly as they flew over it. Margaret turned back to make sure it was still in place before they rounded another bend and it disappeared from sight. Soon they reached an open field on the right bank and Laurel turned and began flapping vigorously.

"This is the corn field that's part of Craig's farm," Ryan told Margaret.

"And Craig has just called me," Laurel declared happily. "See, there he is waiting right at the edge of the cornfield. It will only be a moment, children. Hang on!"

Laurel swooped down and came to a running stop alongside the cornfield. Craig emerged from the shadows elated that Laurel had heard him.

"Now then, Craig! Up on my back! There you go. It will be a bit slower now with three of you."

It took a few minutes for Craig to scramble up Laurel's wing. It was very slippery, but finally, with a hand from Ryan, he settled himself into the swan's down.

"This is better than TV!" he giggled.

Laurel flapped heavily for a few moments and then they began to climb again into the night sky. They flew higher and higher in the air until the pine trees looked like tiny dark dots and the stars and moon were close to their faces once more. The lights of towns no longer blinked at them from the ground. Only the dark points of trees and an occasional moonlit clearing formed the landscape. Then the ground became more hilly, and suddenly the long serpentine river appeared far beneath them again like a narrow silver ribbon winding its way around the base of large pieces of land. At certain times the hills rose around them like enormous shadows threatening to engulf them. It grew darker. The wind was stronger here and the ride became quite bumpy.

"We're in the mountains now," Ryan announced.

"A regular tour guide!" the swan declared cheerily. "Don't worry, children. We're almost there."

After a few more moments of being jostled about, the swan banked and began to circle over a clearing that rose up out of the darkness and lay open to the moonlight. As they descended, the ground rushed up to meet them. Margaret could see the outline of every blade of tall grass, illuminated by the moonlight, standing like silent sentries at attention awaiting their arrival.

"I know where we are!" Craig piped up, determined not to let Ryan outdo him. "I hike up here sometimes in the summer looking for wild berries. We're on top of a big mountain."

"That we are," said Laurel assuredly. "Hang on, children. We're landing."

6

THE KEY, THE DOOR, AND THE PASSAGEWAY

Laurel cautiously approached the ground and reared back touching down with both feet. He ran several long, bouncy strides across the silvery grass before coming to a complete stop. Margaret, Ryan, and Craig tumbled off the swan's back and struggled to regain their sense of being grounded. They stood unsteadily for a moment looking dumbly around them. There was not much to see at first. Tall silver grass reached to their knees, and on the perimeter of the clearing Margaret could see the silhouettes of pine trees marking the threshold to the woods.

"This is where I leave you," Laurel declared, and began pruning an errant back feather that had become displaced during the flight.

"Leave us?" Margaret exclaimed. "Leave us out here on top of a mountain in the middle of the night? How are we going to get back home?"

The swan, preoccupied with the disconsolate feather, finally shaped it back against his sleek body.

"I did not mean to frighten you, children," the swan looked up at them surprised. "Rest assured that all is taken care of. Do what I tell you and all will go well with you. It's that simple. No need to fear. If you fear, the mission may fail. Just go along now, up that narrow dirt path . . . see it? It will take you to a door in the rock of an old cave. You must go inside and look about for yourselves. Take a look at the wall of the dark swan. Then I will meet you to take you home."

The children looked across a stretch of tall grass. The dim contour of a dirt path was barely visible. The path wound its way away from them up a slight embankment into the shadows. It seemed the longest walk any of them had ever taken as they turned and walked slowly away from Laurel through the silvery field to where the path began. The darkness had been friendly and peaceful on Laurel's back. Now, as they began walking away, everything began to look strange, unfamiliar, and threatening.

The air was chilly and persistent gusts of wind kept flapping at the corners of Margaret's sweater. She pulled the sweater tightly around her, folded her arms across her chest, and shuddered. All three of them kept checking over their shoulders to catch one more glimpse of the white figure of Laurel. He stood at the edge of the clearing, his neck arched, watching them go. Then they made a little turn and walked a few feet farther down the other side of the knoll. The descent was narrow and Ryan went ahead. The path steered them through some prickly bushes and over a dead log, but they had hardly gone more than fifty feet before they came to what looked to be a large boulder or rock looming above them. Here the path ended. There was no way to scale the rock, for it was big and looked slippery and shiny as if made of solid black marble. Heavy brush surrounded the bottom half of the rock, so it was difficult for the children to stand up next to it.

Part of the face of the wall was covered with climbing ivy—which, in the darkness, looked like long, thin fingers reaching out to grab them. The rock was so large and surrounded by such heavy foliage on either side that to carve out a path around it seemed impossible.

"Looks like part of the cave," Ryan said, using a stick to bat at some of the bushes that grew up next to the marble rock. "Laurel said there was a door. Do you see a door?"

They all drew as near to the rock as they could, but no one could make out anything. In the darkness it looked as if the rock were full of shadows and deep crevices.

"What happens if a dangerous animal lives down in there and we disturb it?" Craig whispered. "Like a wildcat or a bear or something?"

Ryan didn't answer.

"We've got to push our way through this stuff so we can see." Ryan began thrashing at the brush.

A long strand of ivy bounced idly in a gust of breeze. Margaret saw it out of the corner of her eye and jumped. Ryan stopped short.

"What's the matter?" he demanded.

"Nothing," said Margaret shakily. "I just thought that piece of ivy over there was some kind of snake or something."

Turning to look over her shoulder she realized that Laurel was now completely out of their sight. Ryan looked in the direction of the loose ivy. It was off to their right.

"Gee whiz, Margaret! There just might be a path over there."

Upon inspection they found it to be the remnant of a path made long ago by animals and now overgrown. It branched off at an angle from the main path and descended a rather steep hill. They had to fight their way through sharp twigs and prickly stuff, which Margaret could barely see. Old roots and small rocks half buried in the soil kept causing her to stub her toes. When they finally came to a place where the ground leveled, the tangled mass of vines and branches that had shut out the moonlight thinned. A small patch of starry sky appeared above them. The light from the sky found them standing on a wide mossy strip very close to the base of the black marble rock. Tall weeds grew heavily up the front of the rock, but even so Margaret immediately noticed something bright shining from underneath.

"What's that?" she asked pointing.

They walked gingerly over the spongy moss until they were inches away from the steady gleam.

"It's probably the door," Ryan said and flung back the tall weeds with his hand. As he did so, there was a loud clattering sound and a muffled thud. The children jumped backwards, and a nearby bullfrog, probably awakened by the noise, began to boom at them. Again they approached the rock wall and this time Margaret pulled back the weeds. Nothing but hard black marble stared back at them. The shining gleam was gone.

"It sounded like something fell . . ." Margaret began, and looking down she saw the shining gleam again in the tall grass. It winked at her as if to get her attention. Scooping it up she found it to be larger and heavier than she had thought. She was barely able to recognize what it was before Ryan came up beside her and grabbed it.

"A key!" he exclaimed in a louder voice than he had

used thus far. Ryan turned over the key and examined it with awe.

The key was brass and old-fashioned looking. It had a large ring at one end and widely spaced, jagged teeth at the other.

"Gee whiz . . . well I'll be. . . ." Ryan was holding the key up to the moonlight.

"All we know," continued Margaret, feeling a sudden surge of energy and apprehension, "is that if there is a key there must certainly also be a door like Laurel said. We must find it. . . ."

"And," Ryan added, "it must be a massive door to have such a massive key."

Ryan and Margaret felt their way along the smooth rock wall pushing back weeds and moving slowly along its perimeter, not wanting to overlook a single clue. The rock was cool and in places it was moist. The tall grass became thicker, flapping at their legs as they inched forward. Quite suddenly the rock turned inward. They found themselves in a small alcove with a stone ceiling that grew slimy moss and dripped water. Margaret felt a drop scurry down her back and then another one plopped on her head and ran down her forehead into her eye. She was just about to suggest they should be on their way when Ryan shouted out from somewhere in the darkness ahead of her. "The door! The door! I've found the door!"

Groping her way into what was near total darkness, Margaret followed Ryan's voice. It was very damp and the rock wall she touched was slimy. Large drops of water kept hitting her on the head.

"Where are you?" she rasped.

"Over here!" said Ryan, quite close to her.

Blinking in the dim light she realized she was

standing only a few paces away from Ryan, who was holding onto a big iron ring that stuck out from the wall. On closer examination, as her eyes became adjusted to the darkness, she saw a large keyhole just above the ring and the jagged outline of a stone door in the shape of an arch. The arched doorway was attached to the wall of the cave by two mammoth hinges that had rusted into the stone.

"How can we possibly open this huge door?" Margaret gasped when she saw it. "It's much too heavy for us to move even if we could unlock it."

"Let's leave then," suggested Craig, who had hung back and was still standing on the mossy clearing squinting into the darkness.

Ryan was already fitting the key into the lock.

"Let's just see if this key will work first."

The key went in easily, but when Ryan tried to turn it, nothing moved.

"Help me, Margaret," he said motioning to her. "Put your hands here, on the key . . .that's it. Now I'm putting my hands over yours and on three we turn with everything we've got. One . . . two . . . three!"

Margaret felt her hands squeezed together by Ryan's grip and her skin pinch up against something. She closed her eyes tight and, using every ounce of energy she had, turned with all her might. Still nothing happened.

"C'mon! C'mon!" Ryan demanded. "Keep turning!"

A dull, grating sound of metal against metal began to echo in the small grotto. Then with a loud "CLOMP" the brass key turned over.

"Yes!" Margaret hooted. "We did it!"

"All right," said Ryan, encouraged by their success. "Now all we have to do is get this door open."

"Grab the ring!" Margaret ordered, "And pull!"

To their amazement the thick stone door creaked open with hardly any resistance at all. The low tones of rusty hinges turning in their sockets was like the universal groan of all doors that have not opened in a long, long time.

As the door swung slowly open a melody sounding much like harp music, but bubblier and brisker, began to tumble out into the alcove and fill their ears with music. They stood stock-still in the darkness and listened. There was no way to get enough of it. It reminded Margaret of when she had been extremely thirsty at school and gulped ravenously at the drinking fountain thinking she could never get enough. It was as if her ears had been longing all her life for this burst of melody, as if her heart knew the song already. Perhaps long ago she had heard it before and forgotten. Her ears soaked up the music and absorbed every note straining eagerly for more as the sound began to grow fainter. Finally the last of the melody disappeared into silence.

"No!" Ryan cried loudly. "No! Please play some more. Just one more note. Just another line . . . I want more music."

But there was a hush now, as quiet as the night air from which they had come. No one answered except the bullfrog who was still booming in a nearby pond. Margaret looked at Ryan and saw him run his hand through his hair.

"Ryan," she said slowly after a time, "I suspect that was Joona music, don't you?"

"I can barely make you out in this light," Ryan said fumbling with something in his pocket. He seemed embarrassed by his outburst. "Come on over here, won't you, and help me strike this match. I don't want to trip over or fall into anything."

Margaret looked about and saw that she had gone through the arched doorway and was standing in the middle of a large cave. She saw Ryan's gangly silhouette in the entryway and the moonlit forest behind him. Craig approached the door slowly, still lingering. Margaret made her way toward Ryan just as he lit the match. Their eyes met in the sudden flare of light.

"There's some wood on the floor here. Light it, Margaret!"

Margaret slowly bent down to pick up the rectangular stick of wood. The fire quickly caught on when she held the wood close to Ryan's match, for it was dry and splintery. As the fire grew and sputtered on the stick, the cave slowly filled with a dim, yellowish glow. Margaret sucked in her breath. Both of them stood for a minute looking about them. The cave was dry inside and had a sandy bottom. Old pieces of wood lay scattered about in the sand. The walls of the cave were like the outside had been—black marble but dry, not moist—and the passageway twisted to their right into the darkness.

7

THE WALL

"What's that noise?" Craig asked, standing in the doorway behind them.

Margaret listened. At first she thought it might be an animal, but the roar was constant and very faint.

"It's coming from down there," said Margaret grabbing Ryan's arm and pushing him forward. "You'd better go first because you have the light."

"You take the light, then," Ryan offered.

Margaret sighed impatiently and snatched the stick.

"C'mon!" she said, and began to go deeper into the cave. She knew if she got Ryan to come Craig would follow.

"I don't think we should go any farther," Craig shuddered. "I don't like that sound, and it's really dark in here."

"C'mon, you guys!" pleaded Margaret. "We promised Laurel."

"Where is Laurel?" asked Craig. "I want to go home."

Margaret ignored him.

"Please, Margaret!" Craig resisted. "Not down there. It's creepy."

His imploring did no good. Margaret, undaunted and holding the flame ahead of her marched forward with Ryan behind. The passageway took unexpected turns. Craig reluctantly followed them, but after a few yards his foot caught on something and he stumbled.

"Get up!" ordered Margaret irritably.

"I fell over something," Craig said. "And it's not a stick."

Margaret lowered the torch to see the obstruction. To their horror, the skeleton of a large bird lay across the path. It was yellowed and dry and looked as if it had been there for years and years.

"I'm getting out of here," Craig whined, and in a scramble he was gone.

Ryan just stood there, staring at the creature.

"Gee whiz . . . Margaret. This is kind of weird."

"I know," Margaret said in a hushed voice. "It looks like a bird skeleton, doesn't it?"

Ryan nodded.

"More like a swan skeleton."

"Craig!" Margaret yelled back up the passageway. "Craig, get back here!"

Her voice echoed eerily through the dark, cavernous walls. There was no answer.

"He's such a wimp," Margaret said. "Are you going to leave me too?"

"Of course I won't," Ryan ventured boldly. "It's too dangerous for you to be down here by yourself."

Margaret rolled her eyes in the darkness but Ryan didn't see. As if he would be any help at all should they run into trouble.

"C'mon." Margaret plunged forward into the passageway as the torch flamed backward. "Let's go."

They walked on for several minutes. The corridor

twisted in odd ways, around to the left and then back around to the right. Then they came across several more skeletons of large birds lying in a heap in the sand. They were yellowed, dried-out carcasses.

"I wonder what happened," whispered Margaret.

"Definitely swan skeletons," decided Ryan, bending down to examine them. "They've been down here for years."

"Don't touch them," Margaret cautioned. "They're probably diseased."

"I have no intention of touching them," Ryan retorted flatly. "If I'm ever to go to medical school I must learn to take these things in stride without growing squeamish."

"Gross!"

"These birds are quite dried out," Ryan continued, contemplating the remains.

"Can we move on?" Margaret asked impatiently. "I don't much like looking at dead swans' bones."

She continued to walk deeper into the cave and Ryan dutifully followed her. They had barely gone fifty feet when Margaret stopped suddenly and held up the torch. Ahead of them rose an enormous wall so large that it completely blocked the passageway. It was made up of contorted sticks and roots sticking out in all directions, large shining rocks that looked like black marble, driftwood, dirt, and dark green seaweed. The roar they had been following was much louder here, and Margaret had to raise her voice to speak to Ryan.

"Looks as if we're at a dead end!"

"Look, Margaret!" Ryan pointed to the left side wall of the cave. "Behind you . . . there's writing . . . calligraphy or something."

Margaret turned around and held up the torch but she hardly needed the light. The words were luminescent green and jumped out at her in the darkness. The poem was written in old English, and organized in couplets forming verses that slanted sideways along the wall. Ryan read them slowly in a barely audible voice and Margaret followed along silently mouthing the glowing words.

> Here once upon a time a passageway was formed.
> It led to the paradise of swans, or so they said.
> No one ever made it through, tho' it was tried,
> For paradise once left cannot be reattained,
> Longings once fulfilled and then abandoned do not come again.
> Therefore, beware you who tread this place.
> Leave now with good intent, and stay far, far away.
> The magic of the dark swan is likely to appear.
> There is no passageway, no paradise, no river.
> Only death awaits you here.

It was not the sort of poem that either of them found comforting, least of all the eerie glow of the luminescent, green letters on the black marble. Without realizing it, they found themselves standing much closer to each other than they had before. Margaret noticed that the glow of the green letters made Ryan's face look ghastly. He looked more like asparagus now than ever before.

"Margaret," said Ryan after they both read the words a second time, "I'm . . . I'm not so sure, well . . . that . . . I can go through with this mission—whatever it is. I'm not even sure what it is I'm supposed to be doing here."

"Neither am I," Margaret said shakily. She turned and looked again at the massive wall looming ahead of them.

"It's so big, Ryan," she whispered. "And we're so . . . so incredibly small."

Ryan nodded.

"Gee whiz, this is creepy. I think we should go back. If this is the wall Laurel was talking about, a regular crew of fifteen men couldn't budge it."

"Maybe," suggested Margaret after a moment's pause, remembering something Laurel had said. "Maybe it just looks that way."

Ryan hesitated and then slowly approached the ominous wall of debris. He beckoned Margaret to bring the light closer and she followed gingerly. A large root stuck out in front of him at a right angle to the ground. Ryan took hold of it and began to pull and twist it around. No sooner had he begun than granules of dirt and sand started to spill down from the wall. The root came loose and more sand spilled to the ground making a small mound at Ryan's feet.

"That wasn't so hard," he mumbled surveying the contorted root with a vague amount of pleasure. "It's so dry in here, nothing holds together."

The green letters glowered at them and seemed to grow brighter.

"The roar!" Margaret gasped suddenly, clutching Ryan's shoulder. "Of course! That's water flowing from somewhere on the other side—the river Laurel told us about."

Ryan listened for a moment.

"I 'spect your right," he nodded finally.

"So that green poem's a lie," she said.

"What's that, Marg?"

"A lie!" she whispered as loud as she could into Ryan's ear, hoping the dark swan wouldn't hear her. "The poem is a blasted lie. There is a paradise for swans! Laurel said there was!"

Ryan pulled at what looked like a piece of seaweed and more dirt and debris tumbled to the ground.

"Yes," Ryan mused to himself. "Perhaps . . . perhaps we can handle this."

"And if we get killed in the process?" Margaret said quietly looking at the green letters and shuddering.

"*Shhhh!*" Ryan held up his hand.

A faint high-pitched voice could be heard above the roar in the direction from which they had just come, calling their names.

"It's crazy Craig," said Margaret. "It serves him right for leaving."

"We better go," Ryan said, anxiously grabbing Margaret's torch. "He could be in some kind of trouble."

Ryan led the way back through the twisted corridor passing the yellowed bird carcasses. Craig stood in the open doorway of the alcove where they had entered.

"I've been calling you forever!" he whined. "I wanna go home."

"Not forever," a voice corrected. "Just for about two minutes. Are you all right, children?"

A mild scent of pine and lilac blew into the stuffy, dry cave. Ryan and Margaret eagerly made their way outside where the swan stood on the mossy strip. The night air was vastly refreshing from the stale air of the cave, and on seeing Laurel, Margaret felt herself relax. The night was friendly again, the cave less threatening, and the swan, beautiful as always, shone on them with white light that made the moon pale in comparison.

"Do you have questions, children?" Laurel asked as he examined them both with penetrating eyes. "Craig has told me it is much too frightening for him. You may decide the same. It is your choice."

Ryan and Margaret swung around and stared at Craig.

"How could you be such a quitter?" Margaret asked astounded. "I always knew you were immature!"

"I am not!" Craig retorted. "I just don't like skeletons."

"Margaret," Laurel said gently, "you must never call each other names. Names have great power. As for Craig, I gave him the choice, and you may choose the same. It is better to decide now than later."

"I'm not scared!" Margaret resounded immediately glaring at Craig. "And I'm not a quitter."

"Nor is Craig," Laurel sighed. "Someone cannot quit something if they never began it, now can they?"

Margaret stonily fixed her eyes on the ground. She edged her way over to where Craig was standing against the rocky wall.

"He saved your life, you know!" she hissed. "Don't you think you owe him something?"

Craig shifted uneasily but said nothing.

"And you, Ryan?" the swan asked. Ryan looked at Margaret then at Craig. Then he looked down.

"Are you afraid, Ryan?" the swan prodded.

"I'm not afraid now . . . but that's because you're here." Ryan stopped short. "I was rather afraid in the cave."

"But I am always with you, Ryan," the swan assured him in a sweet melodic tone, "whether you see me or not."

Ryan looked back at the cave and then toward the swan who looked at him motionlessly.

"I'll do it," he said, looking Laurel steadily in the eye. "I said I would do it and I will."

"I am immensely grateful to you, Ryan." Laurel bent down low in a smile.

"We didn't see the dark swan yet," said Margaret.

"Thank goodness for that!" Craig muttered.

"He is a master at camouflage, children. You may run into him and not know it. It is his nature that he does not like to reveal himself. Fear is his greatest weapon and lies his only means of conversation. Children, remember what I told you before! Things are rarely what they seem."

"Laurel, could you come with us next time," asked Ryan pleadingly, "down into the cave?"

The swan shook his head.

"As you work, children, I am swiftly riding the night winds and calling my friends to join me in Joona. Time is short on this planet and I must make use of it. I can do nothing in the cave to help you, and it would cause a great disturbance, I assure you, were I to confront Sebastian head-on before it was time. Nothing would be gained by it. You must prepare everything for me first, and then I will enter and lead all those who wish to follow."

"And the carcasses?" Ryan asked. "What about those carcasses?"

Laurel sighed. Margaret saw the glint of a tear in the swan's eye. The light from the moon made the tear sparkle like a jewel.

"I neglected to mention this afternoon, children, that there have been those who, because of fear, have chosen to serve the dark swan. Never, except in Sebastian's case, has anyone left Joona once they got there. But on occasion, as I have led the suffering swans through the tunnel, some of them have grown afraid. In one way or another Sebastian makes them distrust me and they refuse to venture further into the light. I cannot tell you how it breaks my heart when I lose one of them—when they stubbornly and deliberately brace themselves against my earnest pleading. It doesn't happen very often, but it does happen. Eventually I must leave them, for I cannot force them to follow me. I leave them and they become Sebastian's prisoners. It is death to them, children, as you have seen."

"Why don't they just go back?" asked Craig.

"Sebastian closes them in," Laurel said quietly. "And they grow accustomed to the darkness. After a time they cannot stand to go into the sunlight, and no swan can live in darkness without water."

"Sebastian must be a queer sort of swan if he can live without light or water," Margaret suggested.

"I think he has become something much less than a swan by now," Laurel said in a somber tone. "He survives because he still has Joona water running through his veins. It is his only strength."

"It's odd," said Ryan, "how the outside of the cave is wet and the inside is dry like it was a desert."

"Sebastian only controls the inside," Laurel explained. "A mere mile or so of cave, a world that is not a world, a dark tunnel in between two existences. For him it is home. The rock oozes water on the outside because years of the Joona river flowing through its cavern have never really gone dry. Water is still stored up inside the cave wall. From this end you can still see the water glistening and dripping from the rock. But now we must be off, children! It is getting light, and no one must see us."

"Next time let's meet at the bridge," suggested Margaret. "Away from Auntie Emily."

"So be it," Laurel agreed.

They all finally made it up the swan's glossy wing and nestled deep into the velvety down. Margaret did not remember the ride home nor how she got back in bed. She figured she must have fallen asleep. When she awoke the next morning she wondered again if perhaps it had all been a dream. But as she reached for the comb lying on her bureau, something bright winked at her in the mirror. Turning around she saw the brass key on her desk, gleaming at her in a patch of morning sunlight.

8
THE SWAN IN THE PARK

Margaret reached out and touched the key. It was cool and firm. The events of last night had been no dream. Quietly she got dressed in a clean pair of overalls and tucked the key reverently into her bib pocket. Then she zipped her pocket shut. She felt the slight weight the key made against her skin and shivered with excitement. The key would stay with her all day in school in the dark, quiet recesses of her pocket. It would comfort her when she was feeling dreary and soothe her tired brain during math class. It would be her hidden friend, her magic companion, reminding her every moment of the reality of impossibility.

Margaret glanced at the clock. She had only twelve minutes to get to school. Gulping a hastily poured glass of orange juice she headed out the door with her book-bag half open dangling precariously from her shoulder. The way Uncle John wanted Margaret to walk to school was through town and across a community park. The park had swings, colored jungle gyms, and seesaws set up for children, with a wide patch of thick lawn that ran down to the bank of a small pond. Around the pond were shade trees and weeping willows, with white iron benches for people to sit on and a gravel path that went around the pond's perimeter. Margaret would always walk halfway around on the gravel path and then veer off to the right and over a little hill. Her school was just across the street from the park, a stone's throw up a small embankment and past the teacher's parking lot. The walk was only about fifteen minutes from her uncle's house and Margaret found that if she were very late and ran all the way she could make it in twelve minutes and seventeen seconds. She had made it once in ten minutes and thirty-three seconds, but she was so winded when she got to her classroom that Mrs. Grafton sent her to the school nurse who made her lie down. Mrs. Grafton always said it was important for her pupils to be "prompt." She said the word *prompt* as if it were a drum beat. If you weren't there when you were supposed to, you made up for it double after school. That had happened to Margaret a lot.

"I'm here for a long time after all of you leave in the afternoon," Mrs. Grafton would say, and then she'd sniff in a way that made it seem as if it were all their fault. "And I don't mind having company working quietly at their desks. I have plenty of worksheets to keep you all busy for as long as you need."

Margaret detested worksheets. This morning was definitely a twelve-minute, seventeen-second-dash morning, and she had no time to lose if she was going to make it before the pledge of allegiance. The pledge of allegiance began "promptly" at eight. Coming down onto Main Street, she dashed across it in a frenzy, forgetting to look, and a big, blue dump truck coming around a corner had to slow down for her. Margaret didn't see anybody else walking to school and that was a bad sign. Even a girl called Katie Pratt, who was always late because she walked so slow, was nowhere in sight. Margaret reached the park out of breath. Forcing herself to keep going, she ran down the wide patch of lawn to the gravel path that made a big circle around the pond. She glanced down at her watch. Two minutes to eight. She could make it! She'd slide into her seat fifteen seconds before Mrs. Grafton would rub her red, bulgy eyes and say the same words she said every morning. She would begin exactly when the second hand hit the twelve, in a singsong voice ringing with weary, hypnotic inflection.

"Now, people," she would say, "class has begun. Come to order and let us rise and recite the pledge of allegiance, carefully, reflectively, and in unison, placing our right hands over our hearts."

Margaret would be there fifteen seconds early to hear it all. She would stare Mrs. Grafton down the whole time she was droning on about the pledge of allegiance just so Mrs. Grafton would not miss the fact that she, Margaret, was not going to do any worksheets that afternoon.

A terrific racket brought her attention back to the park. She was sprinting along the gravel path about to veer to the right when she saw someone off to her left, knee-deep in the pond. The person was large and masculine and was dragging a half empty plastic bag of Wonder bread behind him in the water. He had a dozen or more geese and at least eight white swans paddling circles around him. They were waiting for their breakfast and were not the least bit patient. Some of them pecked persistantly at the bag, and all of them were carrying on with a terrific volume, cackling and hissing and honking. Margaret recognized the person standing in the water almost at once. He had on a blue flannel shirt with a yellow stripe running through it. It was Teddy.

Teddy stood stock-still seemingly oblivious to the commotion around him. He was looking at something beyond the immediate circle of birds who were hassling him, with an expression of utmost concern. Margaret strained to see what it was, but a weeping willow tree blocked her view. She knew she would be late if she stopped for one second longer. The key in her pocket shifted slightly. She looked toward the hill that shielded her school from view. She was only moments away. She felt Mrs. Grafton's bloodshot eyes boring holes into her as they always did when she walked in late, and she saw the murky math worksheets with a jumble of numbers swimming in front of her. Then she looked back at Teddy. Alone in the water, he stood motionless and staring. The key in her pocket shifted again as if of its own accord, and Margaret felt herself drawn to the pond with magnetic force. Besides, who wanted to go and sit in that stuffy classroom any longer than was absolutely necessary so early in the morning? She dropped her bookbag decisively on the ground with a hearty thud and made her way slowly over to Teddy.

She was almost at the water's edge before Teddy noticed her. He turned to give her a half smile but then his gaze was riveted back to the middle of the pond, and his face puckered. Margaret looked out too and finally saw the reason for Teddy's concern. Another swan was sitting way out in the middle of the water away from the others. He was a speckled swan, and he was so emaciated that at first glance he might have been mistaken for a large goose. His eyes were watery and oozed a kind of dark substance in the corners that had hardened and formed a crust on his face. Flies buzzed around him and he kept bobbing his head to keep them away from his eyes. The most horrible thing about the swan, however, was that he did not have all of his feathers. Margaret could see large patches of raw pink skin on his sides through which protruded the ghastly outline of the bird's ribs. Margaret thought the swan must have some sort of horrible skin disease.

Then Teddy reached into his bag and pulled out a whole slice of bread, which he threw, frisbee style, out to the speckled swan. The swan was ravenous and jumped for the handout, putting the whole piece in his mouth and trying to gulp it down in one swallow. No sooner had the speckled swan bit into the bread, however, than the rest of the swans, seeing that their breakfast had been thrown to an outcast, descended upon the speckled swan with a vengeance. In a flurry of violent energy they pulled at his feathers, pecking his pink raw skin and his oozing eyes, flapping at him in the water and uttering all kinds of noises in bird language that sounded terribly insulting if not downright vulgar.

The birds seemed to gather momentum as they hounded the speckled swan, and Margaret had no idea how long the ordeal might have lasted had not Teddy quickly reached into his bag and thrown some more bread up along the bank. The swans saw it and raced for the goods, leaving the speckled swan, who was much farther off in the water now, alone and bleeding. Teddy took another piece of bread out of the bag and threw it in the speckled swan's direction. But the bird had no interest in the bread now and was so far off that Teddy's throw could not reach him. Listlessly the speckled swan watched the bread fall into the water about ten feet away and continued to watch as a large, sleek white swan who had just gobbled up a massive amount of bread on the bank descended upon this piece and ate it too.

"So," Margaret said out loud half to herself and half

to Teddy, "they leave him alone as long as he doesn't eat their food and as long as they don't have to look at him. What sort of swans are these?"

Teddy looked at her and seemed to want to say something. Margaret saw tears in his wide, gaping eyes. Then he turned back and tried valiantly again and again to reach the speckled swan by throwing bread in his direction. But all the speckled swan did was sit and stare, watching as the other swans hoarded and gulped down the bread meant for him, bobbing his head to keep the flies away. Finally Teddy was out of bread and he crumpled the plastic bag in his hand and put it in his pocket. His broad shoulders slumped. Slowly he bent over and made a light cooing sound, reaching out to the speckled swan, coaxing him to come near. The speckled swan was not to be attacked again. He completely ignored Teddy's gesture, acting as if he didn't see. The other swans thought Teddy had bread in his hand and raced over in a flurry to check. When they found nothing there, the geese began to disperse, paddling slowly away, and the swans prepared for takeoff. One by one they lifted themselves into the morning sky.

It would have been a lovely sight were not Margaret completely enraged at all of them. If only the speckled swan would stay behind after they all left. She could run to the store and use her lunch money to buy more bread. They could feed him all day, fill his belly, and nurse him back to health. Teddy still stood there cooing, coaxing him to come. If only the speckled swan would listen. If he would just trust them and not be so afraid! The last of the white swans took off. For a moment the speckled swan looked over at them as if considering in his mind what he should do. Teddy cooed louder. Margaret, who was now at the very edge of the bank, called too.

"Come on little swan. We won't hurt you. Come and have bread. Come on."

But the speckled swan, who was still bleeding from the attack and whose ribs stuck out from under pink patches of skin, could not trust. At least not yet. He looked at them longingly, and then with a kind of martyr's resolve, he took weakly to the air following the flock who were way ahead and would not bother to look back to see if he were there.

"No!" Margaret cried as she saw the swan begin to flap his scrawny wings for take-off.

She looked desperately at Teddy as the swan started to fly away. Teddy stared after the swan with tears streaming down his cheeks.

"Teddy!" she begged, reaching out over the water to grab him. "Do something!"

As she attempted to reach him she lost her balance and stumbled forward into the water. It was not very deep but it was muddy, and she had her new suede buckle shoes on. But Margaret hardly noticed. She was watching Teddy. Despite his tears she could see that he was tracing the direction of the swans' flight with his eyes. He grunted as he pointed up to the sky. Then he looked at Margaret and pointed again at the sky. Quickly he waded back up to the bank and Margaret clambered out behind him. Once more he grunted, pointed to the sky, and began to run in the direction the swans had flown.

"You'll never find them," Margaret yelled after him, but she doubted if he heard her.

Margaret was forty-five minutes late for school, later than she had ever been. When she walked into the classroom with her muddy socks and wet, squishy shoes the others kids snickered. She saw Heather Fitzgerald whisper a wisecrack to the girl with the thick bangs next to her and they both started to giggle. Mrs. Grafton raised her eyebrows.

"What happened to you, Margaret Morrison? Would you care to explain to me and to the class why you are so late?"

"I fell in the water," Margaret mumbled, looking down, and the whole class laughed.

"I can see that," Mrs. Grafton sighed, wearily rubbing her red, bulgy eye. "I won't ask what you were doing playing in the water. . . ."

"I wasn't playing!" Margaret interjected angrily.

"Whatever it was you were doing, young lady, that's an extra hour of math worksheets this afternoon. I'll be here until five-thirty, and you can keep me company."

Margaret rolled her eyes and plopped herself into her seat. She wondered if, just maybe, Teddy might find that speckled swan.

CASEY FITZGERALD

Casey Fitzgerald's wife ran the bakery. Casey ran the farm. He was a big man, never to be seen outside of denim jeans and suspenders. People knew Casey from as far back as they could remember, and they always nodded to him when he walked along Maine Street. He liked to eat. He liked to drink. Some people said he drank too much. Others said he just enjoyed booze and didn't get drunk more than any other man. Casey was having financial trouble now anyway, people said. It was proper that a man should drink when he was having financial trouble.

The Fitzgeralds always ate together as a family, and they always ate later in the evening than most. That's because of all the chores Casey had to finish before dark. The night after Craig had been at the cave with Margaret and Ryan, Casey didn't come home at all.

"Well," said Craig's mother, "it's gettin' later than usual. I think we should sit down and eat."

They sat. Craig, Heather, and their mother sat at the kitchen table by the window that had bits of paint peeling off the sill.

"Where's Daddy?" asked Craig

"Shut up!" Heather spat out, glaring at him from across the table. They were just finishing their spaghetti when headlights flared at them through the window. Someone pounded at their door. Craig's mother got up as fast as her bulky frame would allow. Two policemen stood on the porch in the glare of their headlights holding Casey up between them.

"We found him at the edge of the field, Bea," said the younger one. They walked Casey into the kitchen and sat him down on a kitchen chair.

"He's coming to," said the older one. "Some coffee would be helpful. We won't say anything or nothin' that would be an embarrassment. We won't even file a report. But ma'am, please get your husband some help, all right?"

The older policeman patted Craig's mother on her large shoulder and left.

Bea shuffled around and tried to make coffee.

"Clear the table and go to your rooms!" she blurted out as Heather and Craig stood motionless in the middle of the kitchen floor staring at their father.

"Do what your mother says or I'll have your hide!" Casey bellowed suddenly.

Heather jumped and began to clear dishes.

"Beatrice!" Casey continued in slurred, guttural language. "Beatrice!"

Craig's mother came over and stood next to him. Craig thought his mother looked very old. She had a cup of instant coffee in her hand, which she placed in front of him.

"Drink the coffee!" she ordered.

Casey took a sip and started coughing.

"Beatrice!" he said again between coughs and sputtering. "Somethin's been eatin' at my corn seed."

"Looks more like something's been eatin' at your brain, Casey Fitzgerald!" Beatrice shot back at him. "The gall you have comin' home like this."

"I have math homework," said Heather and left.

"How's a man to make a living, Beatrice, if dang animals eat away at his corn seed?" Casey whined. "I'm not gonna have a crop this year."

Casey stumbled to the bathroom and Craig heard him getting sick. When he came back he noticed Craig standing in the shadows.

"Get over here, boy!" Casey shouted.

Craig came forward tensely.

"Have you seen what's been eatin' at my corn seed?"

"No, sir," Craig mumbled.

"Speak up, boy! I can't hear you!" Casey shouted.

He was weaving back and forth. Bea steadied him and brought him to the chair.

"No, sir," Craig said loudly.

"Craig, you and your daddy are gonna have some shootin' fun. Do you hear me?"

"You're not gonna give that boy a gun, Casey!" Bea exploded. "There's no reason for it."

"I'm gonna shoot whatever's been eatin at my corn seed," Casey slurred at her. "And Craig's gonna help me. Arnchya buddy?"

"Yes," said Craig, who had learned never to counter his father.

"I'm not a fool, Bea," Casey whined. "No one can call me a fool."

"Drink your coffee!" Bea ordered. Then she jerked her thumb back at Craig. It meant "leave." Craig left the kitchen but waited on the stairs straining to hear more.

"It's the last straw," his mother was saying. "I'm calling John Morrison tomorrow and getting you some help."

"Who in tarnation is John Morrison, and what right does he have . . . ?"

"He's a physician. He's Margaret's uncle. You're too drunk out of your mind, Casey, to remember him. I'm calling John Morrison tomorrow and I'm . . ."

"No you ain't!" Craig's father roared.

"I most certainly am," Beatrice declared adamantly, "or the children and I will leave."

Casey started to cry.

"Don't leave me Beatrice," he sobbed. "I'll be better. I promise."

"Then John Morrison's got to be called. Drink your coffee, Casey."

After that, even though Craig tried to listen as hard as he could, he couldn't make out another word.

10

THE WALL COMES DOWN

That same night, Margaret and Ryan met at the swinging bridge a few minutes after midnight.

"You know," said Ryan as they waited for Laurel, "I was just thinking."

"What about?" Margaret didn't really want to know. She wanted to be quiet and watch the moonlight on the river.

"Well," Ryan began, and then he stopped. "Gee whiz, Margaret," he resumed frustrated. "I'm afraid if I tell you you'll get mad."

"What did you do now?" Margaret asked testily.

"Nothing," Ryan said, and then he didn't say anything else.

"Well?"

"I'm not going to tell you if you get mad," Ryan said and turned away from her.

"Fine then. Don't tell me." Margaret had not gotten much sleep recently and did not have much patience. Her head hurt her. Still she was dreadfully curious. She couldn't stand it when someone started to say something and then didn't finish.

"All right, tell me!" she conceded finally. "I won't get mad."

"I could help you with your math," Ryan said after a long pause, "I mean, if you think you need it."

Margaret looked at him in utter amazement.

"Why do you want to help me now?"

"I don't know. I just thought of it last night."

"Mrs. Grafton is keeping me after school every day until I improve. Today I didn't understand a word she said, and I was there until five-thirty," Margaret confessed. "What makes you think you can do any better than Mrs. Grafton?"

"I could try," Ryan shrugged. "It can't hurt to try."

"Why were you afraid to ask me?"

"Gee whiz . . . I dunno. Maybe because you would think I thought I was better than you or something."

"You can help me if you like," Margaret retorted cooly. "And you're no better than me."

"I didn't say I was," Ryan stammered. "I just meant that. . . ."

"I know what you said," Margaret continued nonchalantly. "I'm free at 4:30 every afternoon."

"Okay, fine."

It was a windy night. The tree branches bounced heftily and the leaves sounded like the rushing of a shallow waterfall as they blew against each other, helter-skelter, as if trying to free themselves from the branches that held them in place. Margaret was wearing overalls and a jacket, but still the wind cut through her and she shivered. Then Laurel arrived. He swept down behind them noiselessly, and before they could say "hello" he had both his wings around their shoulders.

"Greetings!" said the swan. "A windy night, but if you catch the currents at the right angles it can be magnificent."

"How've you been, Laurel?" Margaret asked.

"Quite well!" the swan chimed back at her. "I've been stupendously busy gathering the suffering swans together. Theodore has been an extraordinary help. He has a knack with the suffering creatures and communicates quite well with them."

"Who is Theodore?" Ryan asked off-handedly.

"Why Ryan!" Laurel exclaimed, and then chuckled melodically. "Of all people I would have thought you would know your own Theodore."

Ryan looked at the swan for a moment and then his jaw dropped open.

"Gee whiz, Laurel! You can't mean my brother, Teddy?"

"That's the very one I mean," the swan nodded. "He prefers to be called Theodore, by the way—although he's not the picky sort."

"What?" Ryan blinked his eyes several times.

"I said," repeated Laurel, "that your brother prefers to be called Theodore."

"I know that's what you said," Ryan responded jerkily, his eyes beginning to bulge out of their sockets. "It's just that . . . well . . . Teddy's not the sort of person that I thought would be helping you."

"Why is that?" Laurel asked. "Theodore's a natural when it comes to creatures of the earth and sky who are in need. He's been working with me for years; quietly, of course, with no fanfare, bringing the suffering swans to me, and helping them follow me to Joona. To him my ability to talk is no different than the speech he hears from all the animals he cares for, for all creatures have a voice if only human beings had the ears to listen."

"But Teddy . . . I mean Theodore . . . can't understand anything. How can he understand you?" Ryan stammered. "He's retarded."

Laurel surveyed Ryan curiously for a moment.

"It's not that he can't understand anything, Ryan," Laurel finally said softly. "Although I'm sure that is what you've been told by those who don't observe carefully. Theodore is simply more advanced than most, and he tunes out things you and I consider important all the time. Mostly what we think is valuable in this world is meaningless rubbish compared to the world he knows. One thing Theodore has always been able to comprehend, that most of this world is deaf to, are the cries of the suffering . . . and that includes the suffering swans."

Ryan coughed and then he ran his fingers through his hair so that it stood straight up.

"I saw Theodore," Margaret blurted out. "He was knee-deep in water, trying to get at a poor swan who was being pecked and hounded by the other swans around him. They were sleek and white, and this swan was brown and his feathers patchy because the other birds had plucked them out."

"Yes," Laurel nodded with compassion. "That was Hector. The only brown swan of the flock from northern Maine. Those swans call themselves the Regalia. (Every flock has a name, you know.) They cannot stand any swan who is not completely white or demonstrates the slightest sign of weakness, and Hector was born a bit frail in the shoulders. A rather closed group, I must say, with a dreadful list of rules that stretches a pond's length. Thanks to Theodore's persistance, Hector is coming with us to Joona this time."

"So he did find him! Theodore found the speckled swan! Yes!" Margaret clapped her hands together. "I'm so glad, Laurel, that Hector will be safe in Joona!"

"Well," Laurel mused, "it's taken a good long while to get him, because closed groups are difficult for suffering swans to break away from. Closed groups, like the Regalia, convince certain members who might show signs of physical weakness or who are a different color, that they were born to suffer and be tormented by the others. Often the weaker swans are so convinced of this they don't even see they have a choice to leave. A most difficult situation in which your brother triumphed marvelously, Ryan."

Ryan did not look pleased. In fact, a scowl was beginning to form at the corners of his mouth.

"Laurel," he finally said with a dour expression. "I believe in the survival of the fittest."

"And so do I!" the swan piped merrily. "You needn't be so glum about it, dear. It's simply a matter of determining who is the most fit, don't you agree? And that's where many have gone awry and gotten it all backwards."

"The one's who are strongest," Ryan persisted. "The ones who can carry on the better genes for future generations."

"Precisely," Laurel said and bent his neck low in a swan smile as if quite amused by the whole discussion. "And those who are the strongest on the inside often have less to show of it on the outside. Their bodies may be weak and frail but their hearts are stronger than a whole flock of white Regalia swans. Do you catch my drift, Ryan?"

Ryan looked up at Laurel and met his gaze. It was bright, open, and steady. His objections seemed to crumble away and he had the strange sense that he had been missing something important for a long time.

"In Joona the strength that is on the inside also becomes visible on the outside," Laurel added with a hint of nostalgia. "It does away with so much confusion about these matters."

The swan sighed and the smell of pine and lilac blew at them in the wind. For a few moments afterward the rambunctious night air stopped its frolic and was still.

"How many suffering swans do you have, Laurel?" Margaret asked.

"Actually, I am not exactly sure yet," Laurel replied after a moment's pause. "A few have agreed to come with me, but many of them are quite stubborn. You might say they're not fair game. I am hoping for at least thirty-five or a few more. Which reminds me, I'm actually in a bit of a hurry tonight. Goodness! I start talking with you two and it's as if I'm back in Joona where time stands still. You'd think time was a swan the way it flies on earth! Anyway, rumor is in the wind that a large flock of swans are headed in this direction in about an hour or so. I must meet them in the air, but first I must deliver you to the cave. I suggest we be off at once."

"Of course, Laurel," Margaret said, getting to her feet. "We're ready."

The ride among the swan's feathers was warm and comforting in the windy air, even though there was more bouncing than usual each time they hit a wayward current. Occasionally, when they hit an especially wild air mass, Laurel would look over his shoulder and offer an apology. They took their regular course flying above the river, over the Fitzgerald's field, and through the dark, shadowy hills. Then they saw the clearing on the mountain, made up of silent silver sentries, directly below them. However, tonight the long grasses were not still and erect but blowing about as if trying to wrestle one another to the ground. Here as before, they came to a bouncy landing.

"Thank you, children. I am and always will be grateful to you," the swan said as Ryan and Margaret slid down his wing.

"I will pick you up before dawn!" Laurel promised.

With that Laurel took off into the blustery night air, circling upward above their heads until he disappeared. The wind whipped at Margaret's face and set free wisps of hair from her braids. They walked up the dirt path and then followed the smaller path down to the mossy strip outside the cave door. Margaret reached inside her jacket and unzipped her overall bib pocket to draw out the key. It had been her silent companion all day, and now it felt good to draw it out and hold the cool metal in her hand. She placed it in the keyhole, and it turned with less resistance. The stone door also opened more easily this time, even though the metal still grated against itself and the hinges creaked. Leaving the door ajar they quietly moved down the passageway in single file. Ryan had brought a flashlight this time and was in the lead. They passed the first bird skeleton and then the second and third. When they reached the wall Ryan rolled up his sleeves. The luminescent lettering on the wall glowed viciously at them and made his arms look lime green. Glancing absently at the lettering, Margaret jumped. The words had changed. Now they read simply in big bold print,

The wall keeps you alive. Do not take it down.

"Who changed the words?" Margaret gasped.

For a minute she thought of Uncle John and her warm bed, and the hot chocolate he had made for her that afternoon. There was an icy chill in the cave that night and she wrapped her arms around herself to keep warm.

"It must be Sebastian," Ryan whispered. "Margaret, I

hope you realize that what we are doing may cost us our lives."

"Good. Then I don't have to worry about math worksheets anymore. Hey!" she called into the wall. "I'm not afraid of you. You can write all the green words you want and I'm not going to pay any attention. Do you hear me? Do you hear me, I said?!"

"Gee whiz, Margaret, cut it out." Ryan put his hand on Margaret's shoulder. "Let's get to work, okay?"

"I think I'll take on this rock first," continued Ryan, pointing at a black rock in the top right-hand corner. "We've got to be careful what we pull out so the rest doesn't come crashing down on us. You start at the opposite corner at the top."

"Okay. But I can't reach the top."

"Neither can I. Start up as high as you can."

After about an hour the first layer of rock had been removed and they had formed a stack of debris against one side of the cave. The green threat glared at them fiercely and seemed to grow brighter as they dismantled more and more of the wall. Once Margaret pulled at a piece of wood and she heard the wall begin to crumble. She jumped back and a small avalanche of rocks and driftwood collapsed into the center of the cave. Still there was more debris behind it. The fine dirt flying up around her made her eyes sting. When it got caught in her throat she started choking.

"Is there any place around here we might get some water?" Margaret coughed out finally when she couldn't stand it anymore. Her mouth tasted like sandpaper, and the stinging in her eyes was almost blinding. The smell of must and the closeness of the cave made her feel sick. Ryan just stared at her, his face black with grime and shining with perspiration. He was breathing heavily and looked as if he couldn't go on much longer himself.

"Sure could use some," Ryan said. "Margaret, there's no end to this wall, and I'm exhausted."

He flopped down onto the sandy floor and leaned against the side of the cave wall.

"I'm going to see if I can find some water," Margaret decided. "I'll be right back."

"You won't find any!" Ryan called wearily after her. "It's dry as a bone in here."

She left him and found her way back to the entrance. The door was still ajar and she stepped out into the night for some fresh air. It was windy and rather cold, but the briskness of the outdoors refreshed her and after a few moments her eyes felt better. Suddenly the small roof of the alcove dripped water onto her head and then the drop went journeying down her forehead. She had forgotten about the water oozing from the rock here. It wasn't exactly a river or stream, but at least it was something. She put her face against the rock, stuck out her tongue and licked it. The moisture tasted like honey. As she swallowed, it felt like a warm, electric current was running through her body. Immediately her tiredness began to drain away and energy flowed into her. She licked again and the delicious flavor of the water exploded inside her. It made her dizzy for a minute. She was no longer thirsty and the queazy feeling in her stomach had disappeared. In fact, she felt quite good.

"Magic water," she giggled, and put her palms up against the rock and felt the moisture absorbing into her skin. Then she turned her palms upward and rubbed her face in them. Dark soot came off onto her hands. She did it several times until her face felt tingly and clean.

"Hey!" she yelled out. There was no response. She

entered the cave again and half ran, half skipped her way along the corridor to the wall. Ryan was still sitting where she had left him. His eyes looked red and swollen.

"I can't do this, Margaret," Ryan said as soon as she came into view. "This is far too big a job for us. I don't understand how Laurel can expect us to tackle this thing. It's so much bigger than we are." He began to cough heavily.

"Do you want some water for that cough?" Margaret asked cheerfully. Ryan clambered to his feet and, still coughing, plodded sluggishly after her. Margaret reached the alcove before he did and licked the rock. Again she felt the vibration of the water on her tongue and the sweetness filled her mouth.

"Out here!" she called.

Ryan came up behind her and groaned.

"I thought you meant you found a river or a lake or something. These little drops aren't going to do me any good."

"It's magic water," Margaret piped back.

"Sure it is, Margaret. Probably contaminated." Ryan caught a drop on his tongue and swallowed.

"Gee whiz . . . I'll say, Margaret. This stuff isn't bad." He put out his tongue and caught another drop.

"Tastes sweet like sugar or maple syrup," Ryan said grinning. "And it feels buzzy like electricity."

"Hey, we'll knock that wall down!" Ryan cried, jabbing his fist into the air. "We'll ram-jam it down. We'll tear it down. We'll stomp it down. Just you wait!"

"You betcha!" said Margaret grinning. "I feel great, like I could climb a mountain."

They did not stay in the alcove long. Both went back to work on the wall after only a few drops. Margaret found that not only did the water make her feel refreshed, it actually filled her to the brim with a bubbly energy she could hardly contain. It made her feel very strong. After only a few minutes of working on the wall together, Margaret saw Ryan pull an enormous stump away from the right-hand corner.

"Gee whiz, look, Marg!" Ryan declared happily, pushing the rotten stump behind him with his foot. "I've been trying to loosen this stubborn thing all night. I just pulled it out as if it were nothing."

Ryan was facing her, and as he said this Margaret's jaw dropped open. Behind him she could see the wall beginning to crack. She pointed and Ryan turned and jumped backwards. The stump had been supporting a good deal of the debris on the right side. Now, dirt slowly began to sift down from the top. In the center of the wall was a crack that had not been there before. It was getting progressively wider and more jagged, and it looked as if the whole wall was moving toward them. Both Margaret and Ryan ran backwards and braced themselves against the side of the cave. The wall strained and shook a few times as if to maintain its balance. Then, sighing wearily, it shuddered and thundered toward them, collapsing in an explosion of wildly blowing dirt and debris. The cloud was so dense that Margaret couldn't see for several minutes.

"Are you okay?" Ryan's voice asked her finally from somewhere.

She fanned at the dust and dirt swirling around her head. Slowly it began to clear. Then she saw Ryan standing over her looking like he had rolled in brown sugar. He was covered with sandy grime from head to foot.

"I think we've done it!" Ryan announced and a big white smile lit up his powdered brown face with delight.

11

BEYOND THE WALL

They waited for the dust to settle so they could see about them. Margaret looked at the green threat on the opposite wall piercingly apparent through the haze. The ghastly green words seemed larger and brighter than ever. The roaring sound was much louder now, pounding in her ears. The large mountain of dirt and rock that had once been the ominous wall now was only rubble. Quickly she reached out for Ryan.

"C'mon!" she said, pulling at his arm. "Let's see Joona's river!"

They found they could easily make their way around the sides of what remained of the shattered wall. They stepped carefully over rocks, seaweed, and scattered roots, holding onto the side of the cave for support and balance. Once they made the rubble, the cave was filled with the same eerie green light as the lettering on the wall. The ground descended slightly and became warmer. Margaret could feel the heat through her sneakers. Still the roar was ahead of them. When they got to the river, she told herself, she would stick her feet in the cool water and drink to her heart's content. As they made their way around a sharp turn in the passage, a steep embankment rose in front of them. It was not easy to climb. The soil was loose, sandy, and very warm.

"It's stifling in here!" Ryan exclaimed, panting up the embankment behind her. "I need another dose of Joona water."

"I'll say!"

Margaret reached the top of the embankment a second before Ryan and blinked in amazement. Ryan stumbled up behind her and gawked. A hundred yards away rushed a wide, deep blue river far bigger than either of them had imagined. Feeding the river was a tall, thin waterfall that cascaded down the side of the cave and gushed in from a small opening in the cave's ceiling. Directly below them was a sandy beach. Two brown swans sat side by side with their backs to them.

"I'm going down!" Margaret exclaimed.

She half slid, half ran down the side of the embankment with Ryan close behind. The sand was terribly hot here and she couldn't wait to get to the river. The two brown swans sat motionless.

"Excuse me," Margaret began as she approached the swans from behind. "Is this Joona water?"

There was no response. Ryan joined in.

"Sorry to bother you," he declared. "But are you from Joona?"

Still no answer. Margaret looked at Ryan with a puzzled frown and shrugged. Slowly she walked past the motionless birds and looked back at them. What she saw made her scream and hide her face in her hands. Then she turned away and began to sob.

Ryan ran up beside her.

"What's the matter Marg? Gee whiz. . . ."

He stopped in his tracks and looked at the birds. They

were dead. Their eyes were red, their beaks hung open. Their tongues, lolling limply out of their mouths, were a ghastly green.

"It looks as if their necks have atrophied," Ryan whispered.

Margaret, still with her face in her hands, did not look up.

"They look dreadful," she managed to say through her tears. She couldn't fathom how the swans had come to such a terrible fate so close to the beautiful waterfall and river. They looked to her as if they had died of thirst.

Before she could think any further about the plight of the brown swans, a strange thing happened. She lifted her head from her hands in response to a mildly unpleasant odor that wafted toward her. Then, almost before she realized it, she found herself shrouded in a dark green shadow that seemed to blow in on a gust of stale air. Ryan stood with her in the greenish gloom and watched. The shadow shrouded the landscape and everything about them with a pasty greenish hue, but it wasn't stationary. Rather, the shadow seemed to flap eerily over them like a cape in the wind moving with hypnotic rhythm much like waves on the sea. As it did so, the musty odor became more and more potent. It reminded Margaret of the smell in Auntie Emily's apartment. Neither of the children had time to react to this strange presence before an icy singsong voice addressed them.

"Welcome, little ones," said the voice, and the shadow covering them made a flapping noise and became an even darker green. The landscape now looked as if a dreadful storm were approaching and the red eyes of the brown swans blazed at them like fiery coals. "I must warn you, little ones," the voice said again, and this time the singsong lilt had a slight edge to it. "Do not go any farther. The water is contaminated. The same will happen to you as happened to these two swans if you even so much as touch the water. Save your life. Don't risk it, little ones."

"Who are you?" Margaret demanded, mustering all the boldness she could and addressing the green shadow vehemently, although she wasn't quite sure where to direct her voice. "Are you Sebastian?"

"By no means!" said the shadow and flapped about them more quickly. "I am Laurel's messenger! I mean you no harm. Drink the water and you shall turn to stone. Nothing lives that drinks this water."

"But Laurel told us . . ." began Ryan.

"Laurel has sent me to warn you," continued the shadow, growing darker still. "He is watching out for you and does not want you to go near the water. Many have been deceived, little ones. Don't go near it or you will die."

Then, as if sucked up by an invisible vacuum, the green cape that enshrouded them evaporated into the air. The landscape returned to its normal color and Margaret and Ryan found themselves standing side by side in the hot sand. The dead swans still stared at them grimly. Behind them the river roared past and the clear crystal waterfall tumbled over itself down the rocky wall.

"What do we do, Marg?" Ryan asked bewildered. "If the water is contaminated we're dead!"

"Let's sit down," Margaret suggested wearily. "I am so hot and my tongue is glued to my mouth. I can't even think straight."

They sat, even though the sand burned them.

"I think we should go back," Ryan suggested.

Both of them looked at the steep embankment down which they had run so eagerly moments before.

"I'm not sure I can make it back up there," Margaret

winced. "I'm going to the water. That green cape thing couldn't be Laurel's messenger."

"Wait! You can't do that!" Ryan said adamantly. "We don't know that for sure. Laurel could have sent that thing to warn us. You could die, Margaret!"

"And if it wasn't Laurel's messenger?" Margaret asked pointedly.

"And if it was?" Ryan countered.

"How are we supposed to know?" Margaret whined. "This isn't fair."

"C'mon, Margaret!" Ryan struggled to his feet. He bent down and pulled her up. Margaret stood limply next to him. "We're going back."

Margaret was so hot she could scarcely see. The sand spun underneath her feet like a wheel. She managed to make it to the base of the embankment and then collapsed into the burning sand. "I need Joona water!" she breathed heavily. "Or any kind of water, for that matter."

Ryan started to climb the embankment but it was so loose and sandy that he kept slipping down. Each time he fell he would get up and try again. Once he made it almost halfway up before slipping down. The heat from the sand was like an oven now. Finally, Ryan let out a tired groan and joined Margaret in the scorching sand, exhausted. Margaret felt his arm. It was beastly hot, like it was on fire. What difference did it make if the water was contaminated? They were both going to die of the heat anyway. She should have gone to the river when she was closer. Now she would have to crawl even farther.

She managed to turn herself over on her stomach and drag her way forward a few inches on her elbows. The sand burned and scratched her arms. How strange that she could hear the roar of the water all around her, be so close to the rushing river, and yet be dying of thirst.

She glanced back at Ryan. He didn't look good. His eyes were turning a reddish color and his lips were cracking. She inched forward on her belly a few more feet. If only she could reach the river. The waterfall glistened as it fell. She saw crystal drops from the falls bounce off an overhanging ledge, and the bubbling, gurgling river danced past her merrily. If she could just get a little closer! She tried to drag herself forward again, but to her dismay she was barely able to move an inch. The heat was unbearable and her head fell limply into the scorching sand. They were trapped. There was no escape. She hadn't known what it was to die before. The green letters were right. They had been stupid to venture beyond the wall. What had made them think they could stand up to the sinister powers of the dark swan?

Once more, Margaret lifted her head to catch one last glimpse of the roaring water. As she did so, something caught at her nose. Looking down she saw the tip of Laurel's feather sticking out of her bib pocket. Her head was spinning, and her hands, swollen from the heat, could barely grasp it. The magic feather. Their only hope. Lying in the sand she managed to pull it out and hold it in front of her. Such an ordinary speckled feather it was.

Her voice was gone and she could only rasp out the faintest whisper of Laurel's name. Again the heat overwhelmed her and she let her head fall back to the sand. She probably hadn't said Laurel's name loud enough. She probably wasn't holding the feather in front of her the way she was supposed to. She never had been good at magic tricks. And how could she expect Laurel to hear her hoarse whispers? She lay there unable to move, knowing she should try the magic feather again, but she was too dizzy. She heard a voice speaking. Perhaps it was from heaven. The voice was familiar, rich, and melodic.

"The chief weapon of the dark swan is fear. Swans have died because Sebastian closes them in and makes them afraid to follow me to Joona's waters."

The smell of pine and lilac filled the air. Or was she just imagining it? Raising her head slowly she saw Laurel standing in front of them with his wings outstretched and flapping. Was she dreaming? Cool drops of water hit her face as he flapped and Margaret felt the same tingly electricity she had felt in the cave's alcove when she had discovered the magic water. Suddenly she was revived, refreshed, and full of energy. She stood to her feet and ran to Laurel no longer thirsty. She looked back at Ryan. He, too, was getting to his feet and his eyes had their normal brown color back again.

"Quickly, children!" Laurel ordered them. "On my back now. We are in Sebastian's territory and it is not my time yet. Tomorrow we will bring life to this arid wasteland."

"We didn't know," said Ryan clambering up Laurel's wing, "we didn't know if that voice, that green cape-like creature, was your messenger."

Laurel didn't say anything. He flapped his big powerful wings until they were airborne and flew over the embankment and back down the narrow passageway. As he flew over the crumbled wall Laurel trumpeted.

"I didn't know you could do that," Margaret said.

"It's my victory call!" Laurel declared, jubilant. "Good work, children! Tomorrow the suffering swans will be liberated and we will overcome this sinister place, for the passageway is clear!"

"We almost died out there," Ryan said softly. "If it hadn't been for you. . . ."

"Ryan," said Laurel softly, "you can know that voices are not from me when they make you afraid. I never make you afraid. I went into the waterfall myself to get Joona water to sprinkle you just now. The water is quite clean, I assure you. Once in the water you are safe from the power of the dark swan and all you need to do is ride the current to Joona. And I would not have left you to die, my friend."

"What about those two brown swans?" Margaret asked.

"They died of thirst because they were paralyzed by fear. But tomorrow, children! Wait until tomorrow! What a wonderful thing Joona water is!" Laurel closed his eyes in contentment. "How I miss that land!"

Suddenly they broke into the fresh air and the swan swirled upward into the night sky.

"Let's play on the air tonight, children! You deserve a good ride and the wind is fun tonight."

12
THE SUFFERING SWANS

The doorbell rang and Uncle John stopped tinkering with a busted window shade to answer it. A woman dressed in a plaid jumper with her hair pulled back in a black bow stood on his porch.

"Dr. Morrison," she began, "I'm so sorry to bother you. I know how busy you are. . . ."

"Today's my day off," said Uncle John, pushing open the screen door. "Come on in."

The slight, intense woman stepped into the house with a tiny bounce.

"I'm Wilda, Ryan's mother, and I've been looking for him all over the place. He has a dental appointment in ten minutes and I just thought he might be here."

"He most certainly is," said John pleasantly. "He's helping Margaret with her math, for which I am very grateful. I'll get him."

"If a swan has six hundred feathers and a third of them are magic," Ryan was asking Margaret as Uncle John opened the study door, "how many regular feathers . . . ?"

"Hi!" said Uncle John. "Your mother is in my living

room, Ryan. I guess you have a dental appointment?"

"Oh, no!" Ryan exclaimed, and slamming his book closed raced out of the study. John and Margaret followed.

"I'm glad to see I'm not the only one who chases after their children," Uncle John said. "It's rather comforting."

"It's hard to keep track of them," Wilda agreed. "Sometimes I think we don't know the half of what they get into."

"I'm sure we don't," Uncle John said, giving a lusty laugh.

The phone rang and Margaret ran to get it.

"I'm off," Wilda said quickly. "Good to meet you, Dr. Morrison."

She waved at them and was out the door. Margaret picked up the phone.

"Hello!" she said.

"Yes," said a female voice. "Is Dr. Morrison there? This is Bea Fitzgerald."

"I'll get him," said Margaret.

"Uncle John!" she yelled into the living room.

Her uncle appeared around the corner.

"Who is it?" he asked her.

"Craig's mom."

"Hello?" he said.

Margaret stood outside in the hall and listened. From her uncle's voice, the way he said "uh huh" and then, "I see," it sounded kind of serious. Then he said,

"I'm on call at the hospital tonight, Beatrice, until about 2:00 am. A lot of the interns are sick. How would tomorrow morning be?"

"Fine. Okay, good. I'll see you then."

John clicked down the receiver.

"Do you have to go tonight?" asked Margaret. "Any other night would be good, but not tonight."

"Margaret, I'm sorry. I was asked to cover for the interns just this morning and I said I would. What's happening tonight, anyway? Something at the school?"

"No, nothin'," said Margaret. "Just in case anything *should* happen, it would be good to have you around."

"Margaret, what are you up to?" John asked, riveting his eyes on his niece with leery uncertainty. "If I come back and find out you've caused any trouble, I'll be very angry with you."

"I'm old enough to put myself to bed," Margaret assured him. "But what if, just suppose something *should* happen."

"Margaret," her uncle's voice was softer, "if you're frightened here alone, I can get someone to stay here with you."

"No!" Margaret said quickly. "I'm fine. I'm not scared. I'm just fine. What's wrong with Craig's mom?"

"Nothing you need to know about," her Uncle said solemnly.

The night was clear and quiet. When Margaret and Ryan met at the bridge Laurel was already there. The swan was in a different mood tonight, not as buoyant as usual. He seemed to be thinking about something and was quite contemplative.

"I have forty," Laurel told them in a subdued voice. "Forty who have agreed to come back with me. That's far more than I ever expected."

"That's great!" said Margaret, and she threw her arms enthusiastically around the swan's neck. The bird seemed pleased at her display of affection and nuzzled his head up against her shoulder.

"Now Joona will live on forever!" Margaret declared, "And the rainbow will grow bright again!"

"Oh Margaret," said Laurel fondly. "I am so glad, so very glad, that you and Ryan are my friends. Without you, none of this would have been possible."

"You're a great friend too, Laurel," Ryan said, grinning.

"We're friends for life!" Margaret whispered in the swan's ear. "For life!"

The scent of pine and lilac grew very potent as Margaret sat down cross-legged by the swan and began to pet his back.

"Children, there is much in store for you tonight," Laurel said earnestly, looking both of them over slowly with wide dark eyes. "There is much that might happen."

"We can handle it," Margaret said undaunted.

"Of course you can," the swan agreed tenderly. "And after I leave you tonight you will find yourselves much happier than before I arrived."

Until the swan said this, Margaret and Ryan had not considered that their breakthrough in the wall would mean Laurel's exit from this world. Of course it had been clear that Laurel always longed to go back to Joona, but the swan's departing had not until this moment become a reality for them. The swan had been available for them, at their beck and call, for three days. In three little days he had become a trusted friend and seemed inextricably linked to them—almost like a new piece of colored yarn woven into an old rug that is not out of place but rather expands and beautifies the pattern. In three little days Laurel had become a permanent part of their world, an unfading mystery, a delightful intruder. Now it was clear to both of them that this moment under the stars, by the swinging bridge, was a final farewell. Margaret's eyes welled with tears. Ryan stood up with his hands in his pockets and looked out at the river.

"There, there," said Laurel and put his wing around Margaret's shoulders to comfort her. "I shall miss you also. But you shall find yourself very happy after I leave. You see, there's a time for everything. One thing ends so that a new thing begins. And I will always love you."

Ryan turned around and his eyes were watery.

"I hope," Margaret said softly "that it's just the way you always hoped it would be in Joona. I can't remember what it was like before I met you. I believe it was awful. A distant kind of nightmare."

"Come now, children," the swan entreated. "I will always be with you. Even if you cannot see me, I will be there."

"It won't be the same." Ryan's voice was shaking.

"It will be different," agreed the swan with understanding in his voice. "But all will be well, children. All will be well."

Ryan walked slowly over to Laurel and looked the swan in the eyes.

"Goodbye, Laurel," he whispered. "I shall miss you forever."

Margaret buried her face in the swan's feathers and let out a few muffled sobs. Ryan turned again to look at the river. The swan began to tremble.

"I feel this loss very deeply," Laurel said softly. "Children, stay close to me for a while. It gives me strength to feel you close."

They sat around him, cross-legged on the ground, caressing the long white feathers that glowed silver in the moonlight, petting the sleek neck, and letting their tears fall silently. The swan's eyes filled and spilled over.

The swinging bridge caught a gust of breeze, stretched itself, and groaned at them. For a long while there was no other sound except for the tireless surge of the river. Then Laurel whispered,

"They're coming!"

They looked up and saw four dark silhouettes of birds with large wings against the moon, high, high up in the sky. One was in the front, two on either side, and one behind. They flew across the face of the moon, and as they disappeared from view, another group followed, and then another and another. Margaret counted ten groups of four.

"They're all here," she said.

There was silence as they waited, and Laurel shifted slightly.

"Children, you musn't ride on my back tonight. Each of you will ride a different swan and follow close behind me."

"Why not?" asked Margaret, who longed for one last ride with Laurel. "Why can't we ride on you?"

"It's too dangerous," whispered the swan. "I will be in the lead and that's quite risky. Children, one thing you must remember. If anything happens, I don't care what it is, you must not stop. Sebastian will try to come against us in whatever way he can, but you must never turn around no matter what. Even if you are the only one, you must keep going. You know the way children. You know the cave. You know the passageway, and you know that the weapons the dark swan uses are lies and fear. Keep yourselves from fear."

The swans began arriving now and stood huddled together in their groups of four along the riverbank. Laurel apparently knew them all and waddled forward to meet them. Some of them he rubbed necks with, and with others Laurel simply bowed low in greeting. Laurel was by far the most enormous swan among them. Most of the swans looked rather scrawny and weak. Some of them were white, some of them had speckles, others had dark masks, and some very young ones were a fluffy gray.

"I never knew there were so many different kinds of swans," Ryan said, looking over the group with curiosity. "Looks like most of them are half-starved."

"It's always the weak ones who believe the strongest," said Margaret standing to her feet. "Like you and me."

Margaret felt something nuzzling her hand from behind. She looked back and saw a scrawny, speckled swan with only half his feathers looking at her with friendly, watery eyes.

"Hector!" Margaret cried, crouching down and pulling the bedraggled bird close to her. "Hector, I'm so glad you've come!" She patted his soft head and cooed to him the way she had heard Theodore do it. "How are you, Hector? How are you?"

"Gee whiz, Margaret," Ryan objected. "You talk to him like he was a person."

"They do understand what you tell them, children," Laurel said, coming over and nodding his approval to Margaret, "but they do not yet remember how to talk. They will remember after Joona gets back into their blood."

Laurel went to the front of the group and cleared his throat.

"Friends, we are all here and are about to embark on our journey to Joona, the paradise that was made for swans. There may be some dangers along the way, as I have told you, but if we stay together and you follow me and the instructions of the children, all will go well. Once we reach the underground river you are free from danger, and the current will take you there without effort. This is Margaret and this is Ryan standing next to me. These are children who know well the passageway that leads to Joona. It is because of them that the way is now clear for us to return. Do exactly what we tell you. This is the beginning of a new life for you, and any change demands some risk. Please, for the safety of us all, follow directions exactly and do not turn around for any reason whatsoever once we have set our course."

Laurel paused and looked about him. The little group of swans stared back at him with eager, expectant eyes.

"Samson! Priscilla!" Laurel called. "Come forward."

Two large white swans emerged from the group and waddled up to Laurel. They seemed, in comparison to the rest of the group, to be healthy and strong. Both of them had dark masks around their eyes.

"You are to transport the children," Laurel told them. "The two of you will fly directly behind me. We will use the regular V formation. Are we ready?"

Margaret easily stepped up onto the back of Priscilla. There were not many feathers and the swan's back felt bony. Afraid she might fall off, she inched her way to the front of the swan, threw her arms around the base of its neck, and clamped her legs against Priscilla's sides. Ryan followed her example on Samson. His swan was slightly larger but looked more lean.

"We're off!" Laurel announced.

Margaret saw Laurel rise effortlessly into the air ahead of her and then with a great deal of flapping and jerking Priscilla was airborne as well. Looking to her left she saw that Ryan was right next to her riding precariously on Samson. He was clutching the base of the bird's neck for dear life and his eyes were popping out of their sockets. In back of her she could hear the sound of rhythmic flapping, like flags blowing in a brisk wind, except this had a louder, livelier sound to it. She felt the breath of the swan behind her on the nape of her neck and heard one of them snort.

They were flying right above the river, following its twisted course, banking to the left, banking to the right, slowing down slightly as they went into a turn, and speeding up when they were halfway around. Then they made a sharp right and flew over Fitzgerald's field. The grasses rustled as they whizzed over only a few feet above the ground. The moon was so bright, thought Margaret, that Laurel wanted to stay low in the sky to avoid detection.

They were almost across the wide stretch of open space when Margaret heard someone holler. It was an angry outburst that sent chills through her. She looked down and saw two silhouettes standing under them, one robust, the other slight. She couldn't see them well, but it looked like the larger one was pointing some kind of stick at her. Then there was a blast and a high-pitched voice screamed. Margaret saw Laurel spasm and something wet splattered on her hand. For a second it seemed as if Laurel hung motionless, suspended in mid- air. Then, he began to drop, spinning downward in a wild spiral.

"Don't stop!" Margaret heard Laurel cry out weakly as he tried to flap his big, beautiful wings to stay airborne. The flapping did no good. Laurel was sinking rapidly beneath them and they were passing him. Margaret bent over as far as she dared and looked back. For a split second Laurel's eyes met Margaret's. They were filled with anguish. Then the swan balled up and plummeted into the trees at the edge of the field.

When Margaret looked at her hands she saw there was blood on them.

"Keep going!" Margaret screamed. "Keep going or we'll all be dead." Her eyes were blinded by tears and she began to sob.

"Keep going!" Ryan yelled at the swans again. "Up higher, Samson! Priscilla! Let's go!"

Margaret felt herself rear backwards as Priscilla frantically climbed higher into the sky. Margaret opened her eyes and saw that she and Ryan were flying side by side in the lead.

"He's shot!" she half-yelled, half-sobbed at Ryan.

Ryan looked over at her. Tears were streaming down his face too.

"Keep going!" he yelled again, looking back at the swans. "It looks like everyone else is still here, Marg."

"We've got to make this work," Margaret shouted into the wind. "For Laurel's sake. Go fast, everyone! As fast as you can toward the cave!"

The swans were already going at maximum speed. Margaret had felt Priscilla's body tighten underneath her when the gunshot went off. Now Priscilla's dark eyes were filled with terror and she was flapping crazily.

"Don't be afraid, Priscilla," Margaret said between clenched teeth, trying to control her tears. "It's going to be okay. You're doing great."

It seemed like forever before they reached the field by the path that curved its way to the black marble rock. Margaret kept fighting back a barrage of tears that insisted on filling her eyes. Everything had happened so incredibly fast. Her head pounded and her heart felt like it was melting inside her chest. She knew the mission had to continue and that she had better pull herself together, but every time she sucked in her breath in determination a sob would escape from deep within her chest.

She couldn't get Laurel's look of anguish out of her mind. Finally they saw it—a silver clearing in the midst of the forest on top of a mountain.

"There it is! This is where we land, Priscilla!" Margaret told her swan. Priscilla swooped down to the clearing and Samson followed with thirty-eight swans behind. They bounced down in the silver grass, and Margaret and Ryan climbed off their swans waiting for everyone else to land. The swans had wild terror in their eyes as they came down out of the sky, and their chests were heaving.

"What do I tell them?" Margaret whispered to Ryan. "They look so upset."

"Tell them to keep their chins up," Ryan suggested. "Tell them not to be afraid."

Margaret turned to face the little band of anxious swans. "Laurel was shot," Margaret told them all. "We don't know how he is right now, but his last words to us were . . ." Margaret broke off. All she could see were Laurel's eyes as he fell away beneath her. Priscilla came up and stood next to her, and Margaret put her hand on the swan's smooth head.

"That we should continue on," Ryan finished for her shakily. "Keep your chins up, folks, and don't fear. Everyone stay together now and try to be as calm as possible. We're about to enter the passageway to the underground river."

They led the swans up the path to the dark marble rock. (It took longer than they expected because the swans' waddles were quite slow.) When everyone had arrived, they went single file down the path to the right and it brought them to the clearing outside the cave door. At the alcove, on the mossy strip, Margaret and Ryan stopped. Some of the swans found the overgrown path more difficult than others and it took a while before they were all assembled. The swans looked very unsettled and their eyes kept darting about them.

"This will never do," Ryan said to Margaret. "They're already scared, and if anything else should frighten them, they'll panic for sure, and then we'll have a mess on our hands."

The swans gathered close together in a tight little group waiting for instructions.

13
THE WALL OF FIRE

"I want everyone to drink a drop of water that's leaking from this rock," Margaret announced to them when the last swan had emerged into the clearing. "You only need a drop or two. After you do this we will let you into the cave, two by two. You must go to the right and follow the passageway down. In the tunnel you will pass skeletons and queer green writing on one of the walls. You will need to fly over a mountain of rubble, but keep going. Don't let anything frighten you, and don't stop; especially don't stop when you fly over an embankment. Here the air gets very hot and Sebastian may try to keep you from your goal. No matter what anyone says, head directly for the river and the waterfall. Once there, you are safe from the dark swan's magic. All you need to do once you are in the river is to ride the swift current to Joona. You will know when you arrive because Laurel promised that the rainbow would be there to welcome you. Are there any questions?"

The swans stared at her dumbly, and Margaret realized that for a minute she had forgotten they were voiceless. The swan's faces had a wide-eyed innocent look to them and Margaret hoped they understood what she said. As if in answer to her concern, Samson and Priscilla stepped forward with great dignity, their heads held high, and Hector flapped his battered wings approvingly.

Ryan nodded to them, and Margaret turned and walked into the alcove. She took the key out of her bib pocket and placed it in the keyhole. The lock screached open. She pushed open the door and the warm, musty smell of the cave came rushing out to meet her. But then something else caught her attention.

The entrance to the cave, usually dark and murky, had an amber glow.

"Give Priscilla and Samson a drink!" Margaret instructed Ryan and then turned and licked the rock herself. She didn't want to say anything to Ryan in front of the swans. A warm, floating sensation came over her as she swallowed the water and she felt herself relax.

"I need to check something out," she told him. "Don't let them in until I come back."

She slid in through the partially open door. Odd-shaped shadows flickered on the far wall by the first bend in the passageway, and as she cautiously approached, the eerie glow grew brighter. Rounding the bend she stopped and stared. Flames leaped to the ceiling of the cave across the path. They were bright orange flames, but as Margaret approached them she noticed there was no heat emanating from them. They were feeding off a pile of dry driftwood, but the driftwood did not seem charred or burnt in any way. The water she had drunk sent a warm current through her chest and she felt unusually confident.

"Lies and fear," she whispered softly to herself. "It looks like fire, and smells like fire, but. . . ."

Opening her eyes as wide as she could, she held her palms out in front of her and began to walk forward. She took one step and then another and another. When her hands were inches from the flames she paused, and then, sucking in her breath and holding it, she plunged into the fire. For a minute there was only orange light all around her, leaping up and in front of her. Orange tongues lapped at her sneakers. Then she burst forth on the other side. She turned around and saw the wall of fire roaring up behind her. She looked ahead and saw that the corridor was clear, and that once through it the fire was actually helpful in illuminating the passageway. She peered down at herself and saw there was not even a singe mark on her hair or clothing. With a sudden sense of elation she turned and plunged back through the flames again.

She remembered how it was when her mother had put candles on the table and how she had been able to run her index finger through it quickly and not be burned. Even then it had been kind of scary though, because she could feel the heat of the tiny flame and knew if she kept her finger in it for too long she would be burned. This fire was quite different. It smoked liked fire, but there was no heat, no energy. It was almost fire, but not quite.

"The dark swan is a master of camouflage," she heard Laurel's voice telling her. "Things are rarely what they seem."

"Gee whiz, Margaret, where did you go?" Ryan whispered at her, as Margaret stuck her head out of the cave door. "These birds want to get going."

Margaret looked at Samson and Priscilla. She didn't need to ask Ryan if they had drunk the water. Their eyes were bright now, and they looked up at her with a kind of starry enchantment.

"Okay, everyone!" Margaret confidently announced

to the tight little cluster. "I want you to know that I have just walked through a wall of fire and I'm fine, don't you think?"

Ryan gaped at her. The swans shuffled and drew even closer together. Samson and Priscilla gazed back at her pleasantly, eager and expectant.

"It looks like it's fire, and it almost is, but not quite."

The majority of the swans stood blinking at her, looking bewildered.

"I think you're losing your mind, Margaret," Ryan whispered.

"You're just going to have to trust me," Margaret told all of them simply. "I will take you through."

Margaret beckoned to Samson and Priscilla and they lunged forward flapping their wings in excitement.

"You stay here," she told Ryan. "Send me a pair every five minutes, and don't forget to give them water. We can't do this without the water."

Ryan nodded.

"I hope it's safe for you back there in the fire or whatever it is," he called after her.

"Quite safe," Margaret assured him readily.

She led the way and Samson and Priscilla followed her with their awkward waddle across the sand and then down the corridor. They both gazed uncertainly at the flickering shadows on the wall, and upon turning the corner they were met with the wild barrier of leaping flames. Both swans cowered. Then they looked at each other with puzzled expressions and then at Margaret. Seeing the roaring fire again, with its long tongues lapping at the ceiling, Margaret could not believe she had been courageous enough to walk through it the first time. It must have been that drop of magic rock water. She hoped the water would do the same for the swans.

"Watch me," she told them, and with confident strides she made her way through the flames. The swans watched her, first in stunned horror and then with relief as she danced and screamed at them on the other side of the fire.

"Look at me! See?" Margaret waved her arms about. "I'm okay! See? I'm still alive. Ha Ha!"

Still the swans did not move.

"C'mon!" Margaret hollered at them. "You can do it too."

She saw some movement on the other side of the flames but couldn't make out what was going on. Then she heard a low grunt and first Samson and then Priscilla came flying at her through the fire. Both of them landed rather awkwardly in the sand and fell over. After shuffling their feathers and looking about, both swans beamed at each other with pride and seemed quite well satisfied by their accomplishment.

"You did great!" Margaret said, giving each of them a hug. "Really great!" She looked them over carefully as the fire raged behind them.

"Not the slightest sign of fire damage," she announced after her inspection.

Then there was a brief pause. Samson and Priscilla were looking at her inquisitively awaiting her next instruction. Margaret smiled at them. These two and Hector were her favorite of the lot.

"We have to say goodbye now," she told them softly. "Fly with everything you've got to the remains of the wall. Fly over the embankment and the hot sand and make a beeline for the river. Don't stop until you get there. Once you catch the current you are safe from any evil magic."

She paused.

"When you get there, would you call . . . ?" Margaret

was not quite sure what kind of noise these particular swans made, if indeed they made any noise at all. She felt that somehow she needed to know if they were safe. In answer to her question Samson stood up, flapped his wings, and trumpeted at her.

"Good!" Margaret told him. "I will listen for that sound. When I hear it I will know that you and Priscilla are safely on your way."

She nodded to them and they nodded back at her. That was it. They took off in front of her and, flying very low to the ground, disappeared into the darkness of the cave.

"Make it!" whispered Margaret after them. "Make it for Laurel!"

Then she walked back through the fire. One young gray fluffy swan was standing there next to Hector. Both of them looked rather alarmed at seeing Margaret materialize out of the flames.

"Hi," said Margaret. "Samson and Priscilla just went through here. It won't burn you, I promise. Trust me . . . trust me, Hector."

She ran in and out of the flames several times and the swans just gawked at her.

"Trust me," she told them again.

Then she heard it. A long low trumpet call from deep within the cave. Margaret grinned.

"It means they're safe!" she told them. "Samson and Priscilla made it safely to the underground river, as you will, if you just follow me."

The night wore on as Margaret coaxed twenty pairs of hesitant birds through the wall of fire. Some of them were more willing than others, and one pair of swans refused entirely until Margaret sent them back to Ryan for another drop of water. They came back quite ready to give themselves to the flames, and once on the other side, made such a racket at their success that Margaret had to quiet them down. Not one swan returned to her after she gave them leave down the passageway. Ryan accompanied the last pair of swans and stood in awe as he watched Margaret do her dance through the fire. By then Margaret hardly gave it a second thought, but Ryan's jaw dropped open.

"How did you ever get up enough guts to try that?" he asked her.

"No heat," Margaret told him. "No energy coming from the flames."

Ryan himself stepped through and stood next to Margaret watching the last pair of swans fly away.

"We did it!" Margaret said. "We did it for Laurel."

Unexpectedly she found herself throwing her arms around Ryan.

"We did it!" Ryan declared.

Suddenly someone was laughing. Not Margaret or Ryan, but someone else laughed, a thick pasty laugh that sounded through the corridor and came rolling down on them with great volume. A sneering, taunting laugh that made Margaret's blood curdle. Quite without warning the roaring fire behind them was snuffed out by a musty gust of air, and Margaret and Ryan found themselves enshrouded in a dark green murky light.

"Hey, what's going on?" Margaret yelled.

"Sebastian. Let's make a run for it," Ryan whispered.

The laughter roared at them, and suddenly the sandy ground they were standing on began to shake in wild convulsions. Margaret and Ryan were thrown face down in the dirt.

"You have not paid attention to my warnings," the voice boomed at them from somewhere within the cave.

"You have been fools, and now the end has come."

Then came the sound of crumbling and loud, rhythmic thuds began to pound on every side of them. Margaret could see things falling all around her, and she covered her head with her arms.

"The passageway is caving in!" Ryan yelled, and grabbing her arm, dragged Margaret up against the wall of the cave. A large slab of dark marble fell right in front of them and then sand and dirt came pouring down from the ceiling. Looking up Margaret saw that the way to the door was completely blocked. Even if it hadn't been, she doubted whether they could have managed to walk. The cave shook in violent jerks and spasms and it took everything they had to remain pressed up against the side wall without losing their balance and falling over. Then there was a loud crash. Margaret heard the odd thick laughter again. Then she felt something hit her on the head and she passed out.

14
BREAKING FREE

When Margaret woke up, her head was throbbing and she felt a dull ache in her leg. Her mouth felt twice its size, and when she slowly moved her tongue across her lips she tasted blood. All she could think about was getting some water, but when she tried to move she couldn't. If she attempted to open her eyes they stung terribly and teared up so that she couldn't see. She blinked rapidly several times to clear them. When the stinging finally subsided she had to wait for her eyes to adjust to the dark light. As soon as she was able to see a little bit of her surroundings she noticed that both her legs and one of her arms were buried under a pile of dirt and rocks. She turned her head to see if she could spy Ryan in the darkness, but she couldn't see much of anything.

"Ryan," she mouthed silently. Her throat was sore.

"Ryan," she tried again, and this time some sound came out.

"Margaret?"

The familiar voice was right beside her and a wave of relief washed over Margaret.

"Margaret? Are you awake? Gee whiz . . . I thought you were dead."

"I'm alive," Margaret managed lowly. "Are you okay?"

"I think my arm is broken," Ryan said. "And my legs are pinned under a bunch of rocks."

"Me too," whispered Margaret. "I can't move and I'm wicked thirsty."

"I know."

Margaret felt extremely weak, and even talking made her head throb more.

"Ryan?" she asked finally. "How do we get out of here?"

She heard Ryan shuffle a little and breathe heavier.

"I suppose there's no way out," he said finally, "Unless . . . Margaret, whatever became of Laurel's feather, the magic one?"

With a surge of hope, Margaret moved her left arm to her bib pocket where she always kept it and reached in. She felt about for quite a long time before withdrawing her hand.

"It's gone."

"Gone? You lost it?"

There was just silence, and Margaret's heart sank.

"Gee whiz . . . Margaret. That was our last chance."

Neither of them said anything for a long time. The cave was very dusty and the air quite heavy. As her eyes became more accustomed to the light, Margaret saw that they were in a very small area that formed a kind of triangle enclosed by fallen rocks and dirt. Ryan was to her left and his back was to her. Every so often a bit of sand sifted down on her head. If her legs had been free she would have been able to touch the opposite wall with her foot.

"Ryan?" Margaret said again.

"What?"

"We're in a pretty small area."

"I know."

Ryan coughed deeply several times.

"Do you suppose we might run out of air? It's awful hard to breathe in here."

Margaret's head began to spin, and she fought to keep herself from fainting.

"The air won't last long," Ryan agreed softly.

There was silence for a while.

"It's funny, Margaret," Ryan finally said hoarsely, "I keep lying here thinking about Ted . . . Theodore, I mean. Of all people! But I can't help it. I just keep thinking about him and about how I've been to him. I've felt so angry with him for so long, I never even gave him a chance. You know what I mean, Margaret?"

"Yeah," Margaret said drowsily.

She knew. He didn't have to use up air telling her he'd been a real jerk to his brother.

"Gee whiz . . . if I get out of here alive," Ryan continued, almost as if he hadn't heard her response, "I'll be different to him. I mean, I'll respect him more and try to hear the things that he hears and understand things the way he understands them. You know, Margaret?"

"That's a good idea," Margaret said, trying to reassure him even though she was beginning to see double and Ryan's voice was sounding more and more like it was coming from the opposite end of a mile-long tunnel.

"Ryan?" she asked, fighting the dizziness with all her might. "Do you really suppose we shall die in here?"

"I suppose we shall," Ryan admitted softly.

"I wonder what it's like to die, Ryan," Margaret rasped.

There was a brief pause. "Can't say that I know," Ryan admitted truthfully. "But Margaret, before we die, there's something I want to tell you."

"What's that?" Margaret said, feeling herself drifting away. Death wasn't so bad if this was all it was.

"I like you."

"What?" asked Margaret sleepily.

"I said," Ryan replied clearing his throat, "I like you."

Margaret heard him this time and smiled to herself.

"Thank you," she managed. "I like you too."

It was hard to imagine that she had said this to someone she had labeled a geek, who looked like asparagus. *But Ryan didn't look so much like asparagus anymore*, she thought dreamily. He looked like a human being. Someone you'd want to have around. Besides, yesterday was the first time she had ever understood her math homework. It was easier for her to think of multiplying magic feathers than numbers. Ryan understood that. Whatever became of her magic feather? She could see herself flying on Laurel's back over wide open meadows and rushing rivers, over long roads and bridges and up to the bright stars. Laurel! The biggest, most beautiful swan ever, carrying her and riding the currents of wind. Then Laurel brought her to the bank of the river by the swinging bridge and she climbed off his back. She began waving at someone. At first she couldn't make out who it was because there was a heavy mist on the opposite shore. She was waving at someone who was walking in the mist. She could see the form. It was tall and thin and had a flowing white gown.

"Who are you?" she called.

The figure in the mist turned toward her and then suddenly stepped out of the cloud. Margaret gasped. It was her mother, looking more beautiful than she had ever seen her mother look before. Her long brown hair was blowing back from her face in the breeze, and her smile was broad and welcoming. She waved heartily back at Margaret and laughed.

"Hello Margaret!" she called. Her eyes sparkled.

"Mother!" Margaret called. "Let me come to you."

Her mother kept waving but shook her head.

"You still have work to do, my love!"

The mist rose up around her.

"Don't go away!" Margaret cried back.

Margaret jolted awake and felt perspiration streaming down her face. Ryan was calling her name.

"Margaret! Wake up!"

Margaret sucked in the stagnant, stuffy air of the cave and coughed. Then, very faintly, she heard something.

"Ryan! Margaret!" The voice was high-pitched and nasal.

"Craig!" Ryan hollered. "We're in here!"

"Margaret! Ryan!" Craig called again.

"Craig!" Ryan screamed as loudly as he could.

"We're in here," ventured Margaret as forcefully as her sore throat would allow.

The dream had been so vivid. She could see her mother right in front of her alive and beautiful, waving. Footsteps came closer.

"We're here!" Ryan yelled.

"Ryan?" Craig called back just outside. "Is that you?"

"Of course it's me!" Ryan yelled. "Who else do you think would be stuck in here?"

"I'll dig you out!" Craig called back.

"No!" Ryan yelled back. "The whole thing could fall on us. It's hotter than hell in here!"

"I've got the feather!" Craig said after a moment's pause. "It fell into the field and I found it."

"Hold it out!" Margaret yelled louder than she had been able to yell up to this point. Her throat throbbed terribly when she spoke loudly. "Hold it out in front of you!"

"Margaret?" Craig called again. "Is that you?"

"Yes, of course it is!" Margaret called back at him impatiently. "Hold the feather out in front of you and keep saying Laurel's name over and over. Go on!"

"Margaret," they heard Craig say in a somber voice. "It won't do any good. Laurel's dead. It was me and my dad out in the field, and it was my dad that shot him."

Margaret found herself trembling. The perspiration flowed into her eyes while hot tears flowed out of them. Ryan coughed. Then she heard him choke back a sob.

"Margaret!" Craig hollered back at them. "It was me that jumped at my dad and shouted when I saw you flying by. He let one shot go, but I yanked the gun down and he missed the rest of you. Otherwise he would have shot you all. He was really mad cause he was so drunk, and he tried to hit me, but I got away from him. I hid in the woods until my dad left and then I went looking for Laurel. He was in a heap by the trees and was getting cold. I slung him over my shoulders. He was as heavy as brick so I had to keep stopping to rest. It took me three hours to climb up here on foot, but I wanted to bury him close to Joona. He's really still quite beautiful. I wish you guys could see him."

"He gave his life for them," Margaret said softly to Ryan.

"Just try the feather anyway, Craig," Ryan yelled after a painfully long pause. "It can't hurt and it's the only possible way out of here."

They heard him begin to chant Laurel's name over and over. The small area they were in was stifling. Margaret imagined the limp white swan at Craig's feet, cold and motionless. Even if he was dead, if she could just see Laurel one more time and kiss his white feathers, if she could just touch his long slim neck. But it was useless. No one called on a dead object for help . . . no one but a dreamer. And the longer Craig called out, the harder she was finding it to breathe.

"It's no use, Margaret," Ryan said after a good amount of time had passed. "Even if Craig goes for help we'll be out of air soon."

"If I could just get some water. . . ."

"Hey! Margaret, what's happening? The ground . . . it's moving!"

"Whaddya mean the ground . . . Ahhh!"

Margaret felt the ground heave and then a gush of water burst through the fallen rock and bubbled up at them. She heard the rocks readjust themselves and one small rock tumbled to the sand. Before she had a chance to react or even lean over and drink, another fountain of water gushed in from the side, and then another and another. In a few seconds they were sitting in a pool of foaming white water that was being fed by five or six bubbling fountains. The large pool of water slowly inched its way up around them. Margaret caught some spray on her tongue and it tasted like honey.

"Joona water!" she grinned.

"We're drowning!" Ryan sputtered as he got shot in the face with another spray of water. "If this water gets any higher we're gonners for sure."

"We're not drowning!" Margaret yelled back at him. "The rocks keep moving, and it feels like we're . . . we're. . . ."

She never finished her sentence. A powerful wave of water suddenly broke through the right wall and hit them broadside. For a moment Margaret felt as though she were suffocating as the water poured over her head, churned around her, and pushed her forward. Then she felt herself jolt loose as the rocks around her fell away and the gurgle of the cool swift current spiraled her out and forward. She was moving rapidly and it took several moments for her to swim to the surface because the current was so strong. When she did, she saw that the current was flowing through the cave toward where the wall had been. She looked for Ryan and saw his head bobbing along right next to hers.

"Hey!" Margaret hollered at him. "We're free!"

"Hey!" Ryan yelled back and hiccupped "I feel great! My arm doesn't hurt anymore!"

Margaret realized that her head had stopped pounding and that her leg had no more pain. In fact, she was moving all her limbs easily in the water to stay afloat. They were at the remains of the wall in no time, except that where the mountain of debris should have been, there was none. Nor was there any green writing, just a green smear on the side wall marked the spot.

Then Margaret saw the river, big and swift ahead of them. The hot, sandy beach had also completely disappeared under the water, but where the beach had been, a quieter shallow pool had formed, and small springs bubbled up to the surface. The whole cave was alive with the sound of rushing water and it reverberated off the cave walls in a melodious echo.

Margaret and Ryan were able to stand up in the pool and feel the mushy sand under their feet. The water came up to their chests and flowed in wide circles around them. The cave was uncommonly bright, and the wet black marble glistened at them from the light seeping through the ceiling where the waterfall began. Margaret noticed that the falls were much fuller than yesterday, and in the light they looked like cascading crystal.

"Gee whiz, do I feel great!" Ryan exclaimed. "This water does something for you. There's nothing like it!"

He paused.

"I wonder what became of Craig?" he asked suddenly. "I hope he didn't drown."

The river surged for a moment and a small wave pushed it's way into the pool and capsized in front of them. The scent of pine and lilac suddenly filled the cave.

"No one has drowned," came a regal voice from upriver.

15
THE JOURNEY TO JOONA

"It can't be," Ryan whispered.

"It is," said Margaret.

"Laurel?" called Ryan. "Laurel, is that you?"

All was quiet. The scent grew strong and heavy.

"Laurel!" Margaret cried. "Laurel, come to us if you can!"

"If I can!" came a wonderfully familiar voice lilting back at them. "Oh children! Of course I can!"

Then they saw him. The swan emerged around the bend in the cave wall, swimming effortlessly upriver. Craig sat pertly on his back. His hair was wet and he was grinning at them. Laurel was radiant. He bent down low in a swan smile and then for a moment he got so bright that Margaret and Ryan could scarcely keep their eyes on him. Flashes of color danced at them in the water as Laurel paddled closer. Then Margaret noticed a large red mark on the swan's chest.

"Greetings!" said the swan.

His voice sounded like the dancing waters in the cave.

"Greetings!" said Craig in a chipper tone. "Look! He's alive!"

Margaret and Ryan moved through the water toward the swan, awestruck, wondering if they were seeing a ghost. Laurel came closer. When they reached out to touch him, it was no mist or spirit that met their hands. Laurel's body was warm, his feathers soft, and his eyes were bright as diamonds. The red mark on his chest was a deep wound, deeper than any wound Margaret had ever seen. It went way, way into his heart. She touched it lightly. Then Ryan touched it too.

"Does it hurt?" Margaret asked softly.

"Sometimes I can feel it aching," Laurel said gently. "But it is necessary for the sake of the suffering swans."

Then Laurel reared back and spread his wings wide and began to laugh. The swan's laughter grew louder and louder. Suddenly both she and Ryan were laughing too.

"Children!" cried the swan. "See if you can tag me!"

They ran, laughing and sputtering, after Laurel, lunging forward in the water every time the swan came near. Laurel kept dodging in between them, flapping his feathers and sending spray in all directions. Craig managed to stay on Laurel's back the entire time, but got just as wet as any of them in the splashing water. Then, before they knew what was happening, Laurel embraced them with his gigantic white wings and they felt the swan's sweet breath on their faces.

"Let me give you a ride, children!" he begged them.

They clambered onto Laurel's back and felt the deep, soft down of the swan's feathers snuggle up around them. Then they took off over the river down the long tunnel toward Joona. There was nothing but the rushing, surging water beneath them, and the cave walls glistened silently around them. The cave smelled fresh and clean. The passageway was curved and narrow at points and

Laurel was flying faster than he had ever flown before. He had always had trouble before with the three of them on his back, and had gone much more slowly. Now it was as if he could have carried the world. The ride was the most thrilling ride they had ever experienced. It was so fast that once they reached their maximum speed all anyone could see were blurred impressions of the cave walls as they raced past. The moist air whipped through their hair, and every time Laurel made a turn the children screamed in excitement and braced themselves for the next. *It was like riding a motorcycle*, thought Margaret, who had ridden on the back of one once before, or better yet, like what she imagined zipping down a canal on a bobsled would be like. Then, without any warning or slowing down in the least, they burst out of the cave into the light and soared up into the sky.

"Welcome to Joona!" cried the swan. "Long live the rainbow!"

They were flying through a vast symphony of color. That's the only way Margaret could describe it later. More color than people on earth knew about. More color than all the crayons in the largest box of crayons she owned, and far brighter. It wasn't simply stagnant color, but rather it seemed more like liquid color because it was flickering and dancing at them. Laurel plunged downward and the colors flew by them. First they were flying through purple, and everything, even their skin and Laurel's feathers turned purple. Then the purple turned to crimson, then to bright green, and finally to gold. Each color they flew through changed them to that same color.

"The rainbow's brighter than it's ever been!" Laurel shouted back at them.

Margaret took a deep breath and the air smelled of pine and lilac.

"Margaret! Listen!" Ryan cried.

Music began to play in sweeping harmony with a chorus of voices so clear that the children could hear every word. It was the same music Margaret had heard the night she had first entered the cave, but it was not distant anymore. The music was everywhere, so close they could breathe it, so real they could almost touch it. It was more alive than they were, and it made the children tremble. The words to the song were these,

> How beautiful the rainbow whose light reverses
> death!
> How beautiful the great white swan whose death
> became our life!
> How wonderful the children who led us out of
> fright!
> As long as we live we will thank you! Thank you!
> Thank you!

They looked down and saw a great body of dazzlingly clear water that shone like glass, and on its surface floated a group of about forty swans, all of whom were looking up at them and singing. Several raised their wings in salute.

"They can talk now?" asked Ryan.

"Absolutely!" Laurel piped. "Joona is back in their blood!"

Margaret looked over the group. She saw Samson and Priscilla waving at them and she waved back eagerly. Then she saw Hector, although she hardly recognized him except for his spots. He looked beautiful. His feathers were full and glossy, and his eyes were clear.

"Hector!" she yelled down at him. "Aren't you glad you came?"

Hector waved his wing at her and laughed a deep

hearty laugh that sounded like the booming of the waterfall.

"Glad! I'm in love with this place! Thank you, Margaret!" Hector shouted back at her. "Thank you!"

They were all there, even the little gray one, and they shone magnificently in the bright light. The entire group of swans seemed larger and more plump, just like Hector. Their feathers were sleek and their eyes, like Laurel's, were bright as diamonds. But then Margaret noticed two large brown swans with large black eyes and several others she didn't recognize.

"The brown swans, Laurel! They're here!" Margaret exclaimed.

Laurel chuckled.

"That they are, Margaret! I told you we would conquer that dry, arid wasteland."

"But there are more than forty-two swans, Laurel. Where did the others come from?"

"Even dry bones can live again," Laurel said.

"The skeletons!"

"No longer, children! When the waters of Joona touch something, everything meant to be alive becomes alive!"

"Laurel," Margaret entreated. "Take us down to the water."

"Once you touch the water you must stay in Joona forever," Laurel said plummeting down to the water and skimming just over its surface. "We'll be passing all of them in just a second, children. Wave now! Wave, children!"

They all waved as they approached the group, and the swans let out a cheer. Then the swans reared back in the water and flapped their wings in applause. The brown swans bent down low in a swan smile.

"Thank you!" shouted Priscilla.

"Thank you!" trumpeted Samson.

"What I mean is . . ." and Laurel swooped back up into the gold part of the rainbow, "is that once you touch down in Joona you become so alive that you are too big for earth. Do you understand?"

"But we don't want to go back to earth!" Margaret wailed.

"Yeah!" pleaded Ryan. "We want to stay here. Don't take us back."

"One more visit before we go, but then we must go," Laurel told them.

They banked and flew a little to the right then straight on for a few moments. Margaret saw a castle rising up out of the mist on a large island filled with lush pine trees and tall, graceful lilac bushes. A figure waved to her in the mist and the figure was tall and thin and smiling.

"My mother!" gasped Margaret.

"I told you," Laurel said gently. "There she is, Margaret. Queen of the swans. We love her so much."

"Mom! It's me!" Margaret yelled waving wildly. "Look at me, Mom! I'm riding a swan!"

"I see you, dear!" her mother called back. "Soon we shall be together again and I will write you stories every day."

"Now!" pleaded Margaret. "Let it be now! Please let it be now!"

"Not quite yet, dear!" her mother called back. "There is work to be done on earth and you are the only one who can do it."

"I don't like earth!" Margaret declared.

"Bring Joona back with you!" her mother called again. "The world needs Joona music!"

Laurel swooped down closer and Margaret could see her mother's face clearly for a moment. Her eyes were bright and clear. Her skin was radiant. Margaret reached out her arm and her mother reached out her arm as they flew by. Their finger tips just touched.

"I love you!" her mother whispered, and Margaret felt those words go all the way through her.

Then Laurel swooped back up into the air.

"Goodbye!" her mother called after her, waving.

Margaret swallowed harder than she'd ever swallowed.

"Goodbye," she choked out.

"See you soon!" her mother cried.

"Soon!" Margaret managed, and waved and waved until all she could see was a glimmer of the distant castle on the quiet island. Tears flowed freely down her cheeks and Ryan reached out and put his arm around her shoulders. Margaret didn't resist.

They were climbing higher and were now flying through brilliant green. The music and singing surged about them like an ocean. It was as if they were being woven into a rich, luxurious tapestry of sound and color.

"I can't live without this music, Laurel!" Craig shouted.

"Take it back with you, my little one, and sing it in your heart."

"It won't sound right on earth!" Ryan argued. "My heart isn't big enough to contain it, and the earth doesn't know how to play it."

"Your heart is bigger than you think," the swan replied. "Far bigger."

They were flying through crimson now.

"Why do we have to go back?" Ryan pleaded with the swan. "It isn't as if there's much back there for any of us."

"Quite untrue, Ryan," Laurel countered. "Things are happening there now that I want you to be a part of.

Having been to Joona once, just think of all that you can give back! There will be a time when I will see you again. But for now. . . ."

"Please let us stay, Laurel!" Ryan begged.

"It's not quite time yet, children. Not quite time."

Everything had turned purple and the music was becoming less distinct.

"Please, Laurel!" Margaret managed finally through her tears.

"Margaret," Laurel crooned to her. "There's a time for all things and I will never leave you."

Just then everything became dark. They were back in the cave with its sound of rushing water, flying rapidly. The contrast from light to darkness was so intense that the children were blinded and couldn't see for a moment.

"My mother did say there was stuff I had to do," Margaret sniffed reluctantly as she blinked to adjust to the dim light of the cave.

"Well there, now you have it." Laurel seemed satisfied. "You've got to go with the flow, if you catch my drift. You've got to wait for the currents of air before you can ride them. You've got to catch them at just the right moment and then they sweep you along. If your timing is off you're in for a struggle. It's just not quite time yet, Margaret. But one day it will be."

The wet air whipped through their hair again and the children swayed back and forth as Laurel swept around the craggy turns with lightning speed. They could see now dim outlines of things. The passageway opened up and the swan took a left turn. They were flying over the quiet pool where Laurel had met them, and then they slowed ever so slightly and entered the passageway where the wall had been. Margaret noticed as they raced by that even the green smudge on the side wall had disappeared.

The water had grown higher and they did not have as much space to fly. When they reached the entrance Laurel flew through the alcove and landed on the mossy strip. The children slowly got off his back. Dawn was just climbing out of the eastern sky and everything around them was misty and gray.

"I must hurry, children, for the river is rising and will soon fill the passageway for a while until it is my time to return to earth. Besides, there is one more thing I must do before I leave here."

"Can we come with you, Laurel?" asked Margaret. "It will be our last chance to ride on the earth's winds."

The swan looked at them and his eyes danced.

"You should be in on it, actually," he said after a moment's pause. "It will be rather fun. Okay then! All aboard again!"

They took off again and flew easily into the breeze over the clearing on the mountain and down through the shadowy hills. They passed over the Fitzgeralds' field and Margaret shuddered. As they approached the edge of the field, Laurel slowed down and came to a smooth landing alongside the road that ran by the field. They climbed off Laurel's back and the swan ruffled his feathers.

"You musn't stop me now, children!" Laurel told them.

The swan walked out and stood in the middle of the road.

"Laurel!" Craig yelled. "If my father sees you. . . ."

"He shall!" the swan declared.

"Laurel!" Margaret cried. "If a car comes. . . ."

"One shall come!" Laurel predicted looking steadily ahead of him down the road. "In fact, we are just in time. Here it comes now!"

The swan spread his wings out to their full expanse and they covered the width of the road. Margaret could see the wound on the swan's chest. It was wide, deep, and red. Headlights cut through the early blue dawn and the rumbling of a Jeep roared toward them bouncing over the potholes and cracks that pockmarked the road. Laurel stood motionless looking like an alabaster statue. The Jeep was not slowing down, and for an awful moment it looked as if Laurel would be run over. Margaret glanced anxiously at the swan's face, but his eyes were clear and calm. At the last possible second, yards away from the swan, the Jeep came to a screeching halt. In a dreadful instant Margaret recognized the Jeep as belonging to Uncle John. She looked in and saw someone else with him whom she didn't quite recognize. Both of them were staring at the swan. Several times Uncle John rubbed his eyes. The windows were open and Margaret could hear them speaking.

"I do believe that's the creature that's been eatin' at my corn seed!" the figure next to Uncle John said softly. "I do believe I shot that bird!"

"It's my dad!" Craig whispered.

Margaret's heart pounded in her throat. Neither of the men had seen the children at the side of the road yet.

"Laurel?" John asked quietly, opening the door and stepping cautiously out into the road. "Laurel, is that you?"

The swan bent down low in a smile.

"Am I dreaming, or is this real?" John asked, glancing over at Casey.

"If you're dreaming, so am I!" Casey muttered.

"He can't hear me talking, children," Laurel said sweetly, still standing motionless as Uncle John took a few steps closer. "Only children can hear me, and only children can work with me, as your uncle did, Margaret, when he was a boy. All will be well now. All will be well."

The swan folded his wings delicately over his back and waddled over to the three children. For the first time, John and Casey noticed them.

"I'll be!" Casey exclaimed. "If I'd a known he was my kid's pet . . ." he began, but John silenced him with a hand gesture.

The children drew near the swan and embraced him. Laurel nuzzled his head up against them and crooned softly.

"Don't cry, children," Laurel told them, "I will be back. And remember what I told you from the beginning, from the first time we met. Remember that I am always with you."

The swan positioned himself and flapped his wings at them. Pine and lilac wafted toward them.

"I love you, children."

The swan lifted gracefully off the ground and circled three times above their heads into the gray-blue sky. Each time he circled he got a little higher, effortlessly letting the wind carry him farther and farther up away from their view. Finally they saw him flap his wings and move away in the direction of the cave, and Margaret was sure she heard Laurel call out a final farewell.

"I'll be!" said Casey again.

He lumbered out of the Jeep and approached Craig who cringed against a tree. Casey stopped and put his hands deep into his pockets and sighed.

"Can't blame you for being afraid, Craig. I want to say I'm sorry, son, for the way I behaved that night in the field. I was drunk out of my mind and I'm going to get some help for myself so I don't do it again. Can you forgive me, son?"

"Of course I can," Craig said in his high-pitched nasal

voice. Then he he wiped his nose on his sleeve and smiled.

Margaret was glad Craig hadn't said that "sorry" wasn't enough like most grown-ups did. She looked over at Uncle John. He was still scanning the sky. Then he looked over at her in a daze.

"I thought I was driving out to find you, Margaret," he said slowly. "I thought that when I found you I would be very angry and send you to Auntie Emily. I came home in the early hours of the morning. When I went into your room and saw you weren't there I called the police. Then Beatrice called me and told me Craig had run away. I came over here and Casey and I talked. He blamed himself for your running away, Craig. I was sure when I found you, Margaret, that I would get an apology out of you one way or another. But now I should really apologize to you. You see, I knew Laurel, too, a long time ago . . . I should have believed you when you told me about him. I should have believed you completely."

Margaret ran up to her uncle and threw her arms around his waist. John held her close. From far, far away they heard the sound of a trumpet.

"That's Laurel," said Margaret. "That's his victory call."